Julie Bozza

Mitch Rebecki Gets a Life

LIBRAtiger

Revised edition published by LIBRAtiger 2019

ISBN: 978-1-925869-16-3

First published by Manifold Press 2015

Text: © Julie Bozza 2019
Proof–reading and line editing: W.S. Pugh
Editor: Fiona Pickles, Manifold Press
Print format: © Julie Bozza 2019
Set in Adobe Caslon Pro and Adobe Gothic

Cover image: © Jeremy Bishop | unsplash.com
Cover design: © Julie Bozza 2019

libra-tiger.com | juliebozza.com

Table of Contents

New York, Fall 2006

One

Mitch Rebecki took a long drag on his cigarette, savored that first raw hit of nicotine, and then pushed open the cat-flap in the window just above his kitchen bench. "Pulitzer!" he called, his voice still early-morning rough. "Yo, Pulitzer!"

There was no immediate response, of course. Mitch imagined the cat out there picking his way through a random grimy alley, ears alert as he sensed the summons signaling the end of his night's adventures. At some point, Pulitzer would deign to acknowledge the call and return home. In the meantime, Mitch threw out the remaining scraps in Pulitzer's bowl, rinsed it out, and served up a fresh can of food. The coffee had finished brewing so he poured himself a mug and took a gulp, before rinsing and refilling Pulitzer's water bowl. He placed the bowls on the bench near the cat-flap, and for a moment peered through the window. The grid of the fire-escape staircase stretched down a dizzyingly long way; there was no sign yet of a ginger-colored cat.

As always, the small television perched on top of the refrigerator was tuned to CNN. In Pulitzer's absence, the screen provided pretty much the only real color in the room. Mitch listened to the broadcast with half an ear and spared it an occasional glance, but nothing unexpected had happened overnight, there was little reported that he didn't already know. He took another gulp of coffee, liking the almost-too-hot shock of it, then topped up the mug before lighting another smoke and settling at the table.

That morning's *New York Times* awaited him. He didn't bother even scanning the front page, but turned directly to the feature story that carried his own byline and photo. The headline declared *Cicioni Still Untouched by the Law*. Mitch gazed at the article with a sense of satisfaction. He even permitted himself a small smile. For a thirty-eight-year-old guy who'd been born in Nowhere, New Jersey, now to be living in Manhattan and writing exposés for the national paper of record – well, that was quite something.

Mitch reached a long arm to grab the scissors from a drawer, and carefully cut out the article. There was a cork-board on the only available bit of wall in the cramped kitchen. It was covered with earlier articles, all with his byline and many of the most recent with his photo as well. The no-nonsense headlines all dealt with large-scale white collar crime and organized crime, and the gray areas in which one became the other. *Andrews Fraud Investigation Heats Up*, announced one. *F.B.I. Arrests Cicioni's Lieutenant*, said another. And, *Justice Fumbles the Ball in Thurgon Case.*

Taking a last long drag on his cigarette, Mitch stubbed out the butt and then stood to pin his latest article above the rest. He contemplated them for a moment, before turning to reclaim his coffee and sharing a smug look with the cat.

The kitchen bench, however, remained empty. Mitch frowned and went to push the cat-flap open again. "Last chance, Pulitzer!" he called. Not that the cat wasn't smart enough to know a bluff when he heard one.

There was still no response. Mitch shrugged, swallowed down the remaining coffee, and went to take a shower.

Mitch had his own small office but to get there he had to wend his way through the maze of the newsroom. The place was cluttered and busy and littered with 'No Smoking' signs. Phones rang incessantly.

Less easy to ignore were Mitch's colleagues, a few of whom saluted him in passing. Everybody loved an exposé, after all, at least vicariously. "You did it again, Mitch." – "Got Cicioni running scared, huh?" – "Way to go, Rebecki!" There was, however, an edgy undercurrent of wariness. Mitch figured he wasn't meant to hear somebody muttering, "He's just begging for trouble."

Mitch waved a general acknowledgement and headed into his office. To save himself further hassles, he closed the door before lighting a smoke.

Mitch's desk – and every other horizontal surface in his office – was covered with files, police reports, consolidated crime reports, notebooks, newspapers, and a few boxes of microfilm he really should have returned to Archives before now. The room was even more cramped and colorless than his apartment. Not that Mitch even noticed anymore. Once he was focused on the task at hand, nothing else mattered.

He was planning to follow up his exposé with an update on the case being made against Cicioni's former lieutenant, Augeri, although the F.B.I. were being even more close-mouthed than usual. The man was being held in deep protection, of course – though it wasn't yet clear if he would turn witness against his old boss – and the Bureau were keeping the results of interviews or interrogations to themselves as much as they could. As far as Mitch could tell, they hadn't even taken any further official action as a result, despite them having held Augeri for five months now. Mitch had gleaned a few tantalizing details, and he could make a few educated guesses, but it was only going to amount to a fairly brief opinion piece.

Busily tapping away at his computer, drafting the article with reference to the scribbled notes in his notebook, Mitch apparently missed a knock at his office door. He lifted his head at a rather pointed, *"Mr. Rebecki."*

One of the mail-room boys hovered in the now open doorway, carrying a package in both hands, a box wrapped in brown paper and tied up neatly with string.

"Mr. Rebecki, this got handed in for you at reception. They said it was important."

"O.K., put it down, then."

The boy considered for a moment, and then placed it precariously on top of a pile of stuff on Mitch's desk. "It's heavier than it looks," he warned.

Mitch thanked and dismissed him with a lift of his chin, and then returned to his computer to finish typing a sentence, a paragraph, a section … He sighed eventually, and turned to reach for the package, which was indeed heavy. Something weighty shifted within.

There was no name or direction on the box's wrapping, no return address, no note. There was only a *Times* Post-it Note and Mitch's name in what was probably the receptionist's handwriting.

The string was tightly knotted, so he cut that, and then tore off the brown paper. The cardboard box itself wasn't fastened, so he lifted the first flaps and then –

A glimpse of ginger fur told him all he needed to know. Mitch stalled for a long moment, and then slowly lifted the second flaps. Pulitzer lay there, twisted into an unnatural shape, making a haphazard circle within the square container. There was no obvious injury, but his fur was dull, and it was obvious that –

It was obvious that –

Mitch shook himself out of a moment's shock, and then slowly folded first one flap into place and then the next. When the box was back together, Mitch reached for the longest remaining piece of string and tied it as securely as he could. Then he got up, took the box under one arm, and went to see his editor.

Tom Lewis was an expatriate Australian, who had not let ten years of living in the United States dilute his accent or his loyalties. He was in his late fifties, with skin that still seemed burnished by the Aussie sun and hair that still seemed salt-bleached. His business shirts were always a bit too snug around a proud beer belly.

There was a piece of Indigenous Australian art on Tom's office walls, and a bright, colorful painting of a harbor by Ken Done, along with pinned photos and postcards all around, and a couple of small abstract sculptures on his desk that were carved from eucalypt or acacia or some such wood.

Mitch was long used to ignoring all these distractions, but that day he was glad of them. In the place of honor in the center of Tom's desk sat the box containing Pulitzer's remains – firmly closed again after a brief examination by those present. Mitch and Tom had been joined by two uniformed cops, and Special Agent Robert Danes, Mitch's best contact at the F.B.I. It seemed, however, that the law enforcement officers felt they couldn't help, or perhaps that was wouldn't help. Having had the matter explained to them, they all stood around staring at the box, while Mitch frowned at one of the sculptures, wondering if it was supposed to be vaguely suggestive of a naked man at this angle, standing with his shoulders and hips aslant and his cock jutting … Surely not. Tom was as straight as Mitch was gay. Which was to say, very much so.

"Report it to the SPCA," suggested one of the cops.

Mitch dragged his attention back to the here-and-now. "Get serious. This is Cicioni we're talking about – you know it and I know it."

"A dead pet …" the other cop drawled. "Not exactly in his league, is it?"

"Cicioni has more imagination," the first one agreed. "Cicioni always had vision."

Tom protested, "Imagination or not, you've gotta figure he's going for Mitch himself next!"

Mitch flinched, despite his own imagination having already played out that storyline in his mind's eye. He turned to Danes, and demanded, "Are the F.B.I. gonna prosecute yet? You've been dragging your feet on this one – that's why I wrote the damned article in the first place."

"Jeez, I *told* you not to publish," Danes retorted. "You throw out a challenge like that, they're gonna answer it. Your damned crusade is gonna get you hurt, and you won't have gotten past first base."

"So you're not ready. Typical. Who's on Cicioni's payroll in the Bureau? Maybe I should investigate *that*."

Danes was obviously pissed off by this accusation, but he swallowed his immediate response. After a moment he stabbed a finger towards Mitch and said, "Times like this, you need *friends*, Rebecki."

Mitch set his jaw and didn't reply.

Eventually, Tom – always the more reasonable man – looked around at Danes and the cops, and demanded, "So what are you gonna damn well do?"

An edgy silence stretched. Nobody met Mitch's gaze.

Finally Danes replied, "Not much any of us *can* do. You know that. It's the same old story: no funds, no staff. We can't provide protection for this kind of threat. And there's no case yet, so Mitch can't be considered a witness –"

"Of course there's a case," Mitch impatiently interrupted.

"Damn it!" Danes angrily responded, jabbing an accusing finger towards Mitch again. "You'd better *hope* there's still a case we can actually take to court, after you stomping in where you weren't wanted and opening up Pandora's Box."

Another silence fell, slightly more resigned now.

Eventually Tom asked, "There's nothing you can do?"

"There's nothing we can do," Danes confirmed.

While the going was good, the cops and Danes filed out of the office, offering little more than a farewell nod or two. A rather deflated Mitch and Tom were left behind, sitting there staring at the package containing Pulitzer. Mitch lit up another cigarette, and took a long thoughtful drag.

Tom didn't tell him off as usual, but instead asked, "What are you gonna do with your cat?"

Mitch gave an ambivalent shrug.

"Guess there's no point keeping the box as evidence. Or d'you want something more appropriate? I mean … as a, you know, coffin."

"It's not like I have anywhere to bury it."

"You could leave it with me. I'll take care of him."

Mitch narrowed his eyes. "You don't have anywhere to bury him, either."

"No, but … Look, d'you *wanna* know?"

"Yeah."

"O.K., alright. I was thinking I'd take him down to the basement incinerator. Not that he's rubbish. But it's clean, isn't it? A clean way to finish. It's … purifying."

Mitch snorted, and found himself cracking a reluctant smile at this unexpected sentiment.

Tom continued defensively, "It's how I'd want it when it's my time. Burn me up and put me back in the Aussie soil, mate."

"Noted," said Mitch. He stood up, and went to stub out his cigarette in Tom's metal trash basket. "Alright. The incinerator it is." Then he surprised himself by saying, "I'll come, too."

Tom clapped him on the back, before picking up Pulitzer with a hint of solemnity, and leading the way across the newsroom floor.

All that fuss took up time and energy. Mitch was used to working long days, but this one became rather more draining than most.

Eventually he headed home, so exhausted that he was already unlocking his apartment's front door when he finally registered the implications of there being a package waiting at his feet. Mitch froze where he was, with the key turned in the deadbolt. The box was much the same size and shape as the one that had contained Pulitzer, and it was wrapped in brown paper and string, too. There were no written directions on it that he could see.

Mitch stared down at the box for a long moment. And then he forced himself to stir, to finish unlocking his door. Once it was open he glanced up and down the hallway, but there was nobody about and there was nothing unexpected to see. A muffled hubbub reassuringly told of cleaning, conversation, television, bedtime.

Mitch stepped inside, put down his briefcase and hung up his coat. Then he returned to warily pick up the package. Again, it was heavy, and something weighty shifted inside. But Mitch had only had one cat, and what had remained of Pulitzer was gone.

He firmly closed and locked the door, and then took the box through to the kitchen table.

Another long moment passed in which he considered calling Tom – but Tom would insist on coming over even though it was late, and that was too much to ask. In any case, Mitch reflected, since when did he need back-up?

He reached to grab the scissors from the drawer, and cut the string close to the knot. This time he was more careful with the wrappings. This time, surely, there was a chance it would count as evidence. Mitch snipped off a corner of the paper, and then ran the lower scissor blade along one edge, then the next, and a third. He peeled back the layer of paper, and cautiously lifted one flap of the box up with a fingertip, peered inside – caught a glimpse of silver, a chaotic twist of red, a smooth gray surface –

And he leaped back in a way that wasn't even physically possible – in the process, whacking the back of his head on one of the shelves hanging over the cabinets. A quiet ticking filled the room.

Bomb. It was a bomb.

A minute or so later, when Mitch realized that the molecular structure of himself and his surroundings were still intact, he shuffled a little closer again.

There was a watch. An old wristwatch, nothing special. There was a tangle of red wires running every which way, with a couple of ends fastened to some kind of electrical components. This wasn't Mitch's field of expertise, he had to admit. Underneath all this, a slab of cold gray stuff that looked malleable was surely a block of explosive. It was classic, really.

The watch continued ticking. Mitch leaned a little closer, wondering if he could make out when it was due to go off, how much time he had, whether he should get the damned thing out of the building or try to evacuate his neighbors …

How was it going to work? Was the minute hand going to trigger the explosion next time it hit twelve, or what? Mitch frowned. Was that even possible, with an old analog wristwatch … ? Surely not.

He edged closer, and then carefully reached in to shift the watch a little.

And realized it wasn't actually connected to anything. Like the wires. They were sitting there loose. He lifted them free, just to be sure. The slab of whatever it was – could it be something harmless, like putty? – sat there looking distinctly shame-faced.

Mitch took his first proper breath for some while, and let himself sag in relief.

Still. It was the makings of a bomb. And Mitch knew who'd sent it. Even if the first message had left room in which the skeptics doubted, this second one definitely clarified matters.

Mitch grabbed his phone, and thumbed through the contact list for Special Agent Danes.

Soon Danes and a different pair of uniformed cops were crammed into the tiny kitchen with Mitch. He'd called Tom, but insisted on him not bothering to come around. The law enforcement officers weren't being all that much more helpful than before, but at least they were treating this package as evidence. They examined it all while being careful not to touch anything, peering and staring, and then exchanging cryptic remarks between themselves. Eventually one of the cops took a few photographs before they donned plastic gloves and eased the whole shebang into a plastic bag.

Mitch was sitting with his chair backed up against the cabinets, as far out of the way as he could be. Which wasn't far. He was, at this point, feeling seriously irritated – a condition which wasn't ameliorated even by fresh coffee and cigarettes. He hadn't offered coffee to the others, and consciousness of that was also putting him out of sorts, but they'd been muttering between themselves at the time and none of them had even lifted his or her head.

Eventually, when the evidence was good to go, Danes looked levelly at Mitch for a moment before saying, "I wouldn't expect too much."

Mitch gaped at him, then blurted out, "You're kidding me! This isn't serious enough yet?"

"We'll look into it," Danes said in his most reasonable calm-the-witness tones, "but it won't do us much good. Most of this you can buy at any hardware store. Even the watch – it's old, but it's nothing special. It's not likely to be traceable. We'd have had a better chance if that *had* been C4."

"Oh, right," said Mitch with his sarcasm turned up to eleven. "Sure. That would have been great."

"But if it's Cicioni," Danes continued, overriding him. "You know, he ain't gonna let himself get caught over something like this."

"He's escalating. Next time it might be wired up."

Danes let out a sigh, and then turned to consider the two cops. "Well, realistically … I can ask for these two to park out front of your building tonight. We can assign a pair of uniforms to keep close to you for, say, forty-eight hours. But that's about it."

"Oh, yeah," said Mitch. "Wonderful. Thanks."

The two cops looked about as unimpressed as Mitch was himself.

Finally Mitch was alone again, but even that didn't cheer him up. He felt utterly deflated. He went to change into his pajamas and robe, and then returned to set the kitchen to rights. Rinsing out his mug and the jug from the drip coffee maker took a moment, as did discarding the ground coffee and the filter. Then, as he did on most nights, Mitch picked up Pulitzer's bowl, and dropped the contents in the trash. Of course, it was rather more than usual. Pulitzer rarely left anything more than scraps behind. Mitch set his jaw, picked up the water bowl, and poured the remaining water down the sink.

He was just about to rinse out the bowls when he had a change of heart. He stared down at them for a long moment. And then he very deliberately picked up the food bowl again, and dumped it in the trash. A breath snagged in his throat. He caught up the water bowl, and dumped that as well. His hand jerked away in a dramatic flourish as if it hardly even belonged to him.

His breath was coming hard now, so he took a moment. He leaned both hands on the cold metal rim of the sink, and reached to retrieve his equilibrium from wherever it had run off to. Surprisingly, this took several minutes.

But eventually Mitch was calm again. He let out a sigh before turning away, switching off the light, and heading for his bed.

The next morning, Mitch arrived at work to find a note on his desk – in

Tom's own handwriting – directing him to Tom's office 'ASAP'. This was followed, in the typically understated Australian way, with three exclamation marks. Mitch shrugged, put his satchel down on his desk, and went to obey.

If Mitch had expected Tom to be angry and concerned about the bomb that hadn't after all been a bomb, he was disappointed. Instead Tom seemed to be bubbling over with excitement. His eyes were sparking, so much so that Mitch worried vaguely about electrical fires. Tom even stood from his desk, and came to usher Mitch to a seat, before closing the door.

"I've got an idea," Tom announced. "A great idea, a wonderful idea …"

Mitch was too numb to respond in kind. He nodded, indicating he was willing to hear what Tom was obviously dying to tell him.

"I really miss home," said Tom, rather unexpectedly. "You've never been to Australia, right?"

Mitch shook his head, wondering where the fuck that came from.

"You should go. The people, the sunshine, the beaches, the splendor …" Tom looked about him at the artwork, the postcards, as if seeking inspiration. Which he must have found, because it then spilled forth: "The soil in the Outback can be as rich and red as blood, like the land is bleeding. The ocean's an opal come to life. The sand's either the *purest* white or gold-dust, and –"

Mitch *so* wasn't in the mood. "Very poetic. But I'm not interested in a vacation, Tom."

"I'm not talking about a holiday, mate," Tom replied in more reasonable tones. "I'm talking about you going underground for a while, keeping your head down until it's safe here. You can work for my cousin Eva, she's editor for the *Herald* in Sydney."

Not a chance in hell. "I don't think so," said Mitch.

Tom, of course, sailed right on. "You'll need to be clever about this, it's like going undercover. You can write under a pseudonym – and leave the investigative journalism behind for a while."

"What? But that's all I –" He only just managed to stop himself in time. *That's all I have. That's all I know.* Mitch gathered himself, and came up with an argument that he could live with, that any New Yorker would understand. "Yeah, great, Tom, but the fact is I can't afford to pick up and go live overseas. My rent swallows up most of my salary, and you can't expect me to let a Manhattan apartment go."

Unfortunately that just made Tom's eyes spark again. It was as if he were in love with his own idea. "I thought about that."

"Great."

"You work part-time for Eva, and she'll pay you accordingly. Plus you write weekly lifestyle pieces about Australia for our Sunday magazine –" Tom waved a sample of the glossy supplement, as if Mitch hadn't thrown it in the trash a thousand times already – "and I'll continue your salary. I'll even pay your airfare and some of your living expenses." He concluded triumphantly, "What d'you think about *that*?"

Mitch rolled his eyes at the sheer indignity of it all. "*Lifestyle* pieces, my God … I'm better than that, Tom. I've always been better than that."

Tom sagged just enough to acknowledge the assertion. "I know, I really do, but that's not the point. I've cleared it with Gail – you heard she's editing the magazine now? She's O.K. with you contributing –"

"O.K.? She should be flattered! But you wanna exile me from everything that's civilized? I ain't ready for a sabbatical, Tom!"

"Do you even have a choice right now? Don't tell me you'd rather get your head blown off, and let Cicioni walk away Scot-free."

"I can't walk away from this," Mitch insisted. He leaned forward to add, "I can't walk away from what I do. You should know that, Tom."

"Mitch, it's just getting too dangerous right now."

"All the more reason to see it through!"

"It's not like you're a cop on a case," Tom argued.

"No! I'm a journalist on a story. A *serious* journalist on an *important* story."

"The story will wait!"

Mitch stared at the man. "Said no editor *ever*."

Tom shot him a grumpy glare. "Let Danes do his job." And then he cried out in frustration, "Leave it alone, Mitch! Go to Australia. Try something new. Oh, yeah – and while you're at it – *get a life!*"

Mitch opened his mouth to retort, but he had nothing. So he closed it again, and sank down in the chair. He felt as winded as if he'd just taken a blow to the gut.

Not unexpectedly, Tom gently yet relentlessly pressed home his advantage. "You don't have a choice, Mitch. Anyway, it only has to be until the Feds are ready to prosecute, then you're not a lone crusader anymore. Then you can come back and cover the trial, alright?"

Mitch didn't reply. He looked glumly at Tom, and then dropped his gaze, reluctantly beginning to wonder if this was indeed the way it had to be.

He didn't exactly get much work done that morning. He didn't achieve anything beyond smoking so many cigarettes that even he was starting to find the atmosphere in his office a bit oxygen-starved.

Eventually, around midday, Mitch came to a decision. He stubbed out the butt of the last smoke he had with him, crushed the empty packet and tossed it in the trash, then picked up his phone and thumbed through the recent calls list.

Barely time for one ring, and the call was picked up. "F.B.I., Agent Danes speaking."

"It's Mitch Rebecki," he said. "I'm gonna get out of harm's way for a while. Discretion being the better part of valor, right?"

"That's good, Rebecki." Danes didn't exactly sound surprised, which made Mitch suspect that Tom must have already spoken to him. "We'll all still be here when you get back," Danes was reassuring him. "I'm hoping Cicioni will be off the streets, though."

"Right." Mitch's hackles were up at the feeling of being managed, but he forced them back down or at least into their regular configuration. "I need a favor, though, Danes. I want a passport in a different name. I'm not expecting a whole new identity or anything. Just enough so I can hide in plain sight and not worry about it, you know?"

Danes hardly even left a beat before replying, "I guess we can do that. If you'll let us have your file on Cicioni."

Mitch huffed out a breath. "God, you don't ask for much, do you?" Again, however, the decision soon seemed inevitable. "O.K. You can pick it up when you bring me the passport. Make the name Martin Delmonaco. He was my mom's father."

"That name's too close to home, Mitch. You need something plausible and ordinary, that doesn't lead right back to you."

But Mitch just laughed. "You know Tom's sending me Down Under, right? He probably wants to come, too."

"Wouldn't mind it myself," said Danes.

"Yeah, but nobody's gonna come looking for me there, are they? One of their own prime ministers called the country 'the arse end of the world'. Don't sweat it. Nothing ever happens in Australia."

Sydney, Spring and Summer 2006

Two

The six-hour flight from New York to L.A. was bad enough, and the two-hour layover gave Mitch barely enough time to transfer planes let alone catch up on caffeine and nicotine. The fifteen-hour flight to Sydney was absolutely hellish. And of course even once they'd landed, there was passport control to get through, and Mitch had heard that the Australian Quarantine and Inspection Service took their job a bit too seriously. Most airports these days just let you breeze through the Nothing to Declare gate, but not AQIS, no.

Not that Mitch had even got that far yet. He was standing in one of the many long lines awaiting the attention of an Immigration Officer. His journalist's eye told him the place was clean and the atmosphere was efficient. It was true that the queues were steadily if slowly moving, though naturally the line he'd been directed to was slowest of all. His fellow travelers seemed tired yet patient. But not Mitch. He was exhausted. He hadn't slept on the flight, and if his body clock was keeping the correct time it must be the small hours of the night for him. He was cold to the point of an occasional tremble. Not to mention that he felt generally seedy, and sweaty in a whole bunch of rather uncomfortable places. All of which was on top of the constant low-level anger about even being here at all. And oh God he was honestly literally prepared to kill for a smoke right now.

But at last Mitch was at the head of the line, and then finally at long fucking last he was beckoned forward by an Immigration Officer. Mitch rolled his eyes in mock relief, stepped up to the desk, and handed over his passport and the completed entry form.

"Good morning, sir," the Immigration Officer said.

Mitch mumbled a monosyllabic response, and tried not to remark on how odd it was to hear an Australian accent using a polite tone. Maybe he was just too used to Tom's gruff ways.

The officer examined the passport, compared Mitch to the photo, and then ran the passport number through his computer. He took a few long moments to consider the information brought up on the screen. Eventually he asked, "You're Martin Delmonaco?"

"That's what it says," Mitch replied. He squinted at the guy's security badge. "And you're James Toller?"

"Yes, sir," came the smooth reply, unruffled by sarcasm. Toller continued, "Have you traveled outside the United States before?"

"Yeah, sure."

The officer turned his head to consider Mitch with an unruffled calm. He was so irritatingly Zen. "There's no immigration history against this passport, sir. It's brand new. And there's no record of you having a previous passport."

Mitch grimaced in utter exasperation, before he managed to remind himself to rein in the attitude. Still, that bastard Danes could have organized something a bit more realistic. Mitch scrambled to recover the lost ground. "Well, uh … I mean, I've been to Canada a lot. For my sins, you know? They don't want to check your passport if you're a U.S. citizen," he babbled on. "All they do is look at your driver's license."

A cool smile stretched the officer's mouth but didn't show in his eyes.

Mitch tried not to betray anxiety as he realized he shouldn't have gotten into that much detail. If the officer now asked to see the said driver's license, Mitch would have to confess to letting it lapse since he'd moved to New York City.

It seemed, however, that they could safely move on to the next topic of conversation. "Are you here for business or pleasure, sir?"

Mitch felt almost lightheaded with relief. "*Pleasure?* You're kidding me. Strictly business."

His interrogator didn't even blink. "What kind of business?"

"I'm a journalist. I'll be working from the *Sydney Morning Herald* offices, sending stories back to civilization, otherwise known as New York."

The Immigration Officer let a well-judged beat go by before asking, "And you didn't have a working visa approved before you left?"

An irresistible surge of serious disgruntlement coursed through him. "There wasn't time, alright? My boss back in New York will have submitted the paperwork by now. And you know what?" he continued despite knowing it was unwise. "It's all getting pushed through by somebody considerably above your pay-grade in the F.B.-fucking-I."

Another cool, polite smile was directed towards Mitch even while the

Immigration Officer discreetly beckoned over a colleague. Mitch wasn't so furious – yet – that he didn't register the newcomer as a rather attractive Indigenous Australian who looked totally fit in his crisply pressed white shirt and taupe pants.

Mitch peered at the Custom Officer's badge, and read out his name. "Samuel Windrayne. Is that how you pronounce it? Wind-rain?"

"Yes, sir," the man replied, deadpan but for the slightest glint of humor in his dark eyes.

The Immigration Officer was smoothly continuing, "We'll take the time to follow up your visa now, sir, while Customs conduct a full search of your luggage and your person."

Mitch tore his gaze away from the rather distracting Samuel Windrayne. "My person?! If that means what the fuck I think it means, you can think again."

Despite which Windrayne led Mitch off towards a set of double doors, with Mitch protesting all the way. He was vaguely aware of the other travelers averting their gazes and trying to ignore the fuss, or watching with a horrified kind of fascination. One thing Mitch was certain about was that, guilty or innocent, everybody there was glad it was him and not them.

"What the hell's *wrong* with you people? Can't you tell an actual criminal when you see one? You should come to America and take some lessons from real Immigration and Customs Officers. There's probably a dozen dope smugglers waiting in line right now, laughing at how easy it is to fool you all …"

Mitch was seething. His dignity was in tatters after the most humiliating hour of his life. He was now at last getting dressed again, though still under the watchful eye of the Customs Officer, Samuel Windrayne. The room was small – and cold and bare – but Mitch tried to keep his distance as much as possible. It had only added insult to injury to be naked while so badly in need of a shower, when his only witness was this young man who was not only attractive but smart as a new day.

Mitch's two suitcases were lying open on a table, with their contents scattered. Waiting for the cases to be brought to the room had taken up much of the hour, though at least he'd been given a coffee to tide him over.

And he'd been saved the hassle of Baggage Claim, though that was a consolation so small as to be almost nonexistent. It was only once the baggage guy had left, that Windrayne had locked the door and required Mitch to strip.

When Mitch was dressed again – in the same clothes he'd worn for well over twenty-four hours now – he started repacking one of the cases. Despite the fact that good quality clothes were the one luxury Mitch allowed himself, he was too angry to be neat. After a moment Windrayne stripped off the surgical gloves he was still wearing, and stepped up to help by repacking the other case.

Mitch stopped him with a glare. "Don't you think you've touched enough?"

The young man paused.

Mitch leaned close, got right in his face, and said in tones that were both furious and insinuating, "Next time you want to get intimate with me, you buy me a drink first."

At first the Customs Officer managed to maintain his official poker face. But finally he was ambushed by a smile – an amused and slightly suggestive smile. His dark brown gaze was warm and direct. "Yes, sir."

For a moment, Mitch was completely disarmed. There was no denying that on any other day he'd have been pleased to make this man's acquaintance.

But not that day. Mitch shook himself, and withdrew into another glare, while Windrayne returned to his poker-faced official self. Feeling the anger roil dully in his gut, Mitch finished the shambolic repacking, and within moments he was stalking out the door.

"Welcome to Australia," said the security guard who finally let him out into the fresh air.

Mitch was only prevented from swearing by the thought of suffering through another interrogation. He just growled, and reached for his cigarettes.

The newspaper offices were in one of those modern, spacious buildings with lots of glass spun across shining threads of steel. The place was full to overflowing with natural light, and bright Australian light at that; far too much of the stuff for somebody suffering from sleep deprivation. Mitch sensed the beginnings of a killer headache lurking ready to pounce.

He'd checked into the hotel that had been booked for him and, with a rare sense of eternal gratitude had had a long shower. The huge bed with its crisp white linen had looked incredibly tempting, but he'd refused to surrender. He was not going to spend his day napping like an octogenarian. The only way to deal with jet-lag, Mitch knew, was to force his way through it.

So now he was stalking through the bustling newsroom, feeling a little edgier than he'd like. He was following some random employee the security guard had roped in to escort him, and they were heading for the editor's office. At the earliest opportunity the employee indicated the office, and with a wave indicated that Mitch could make his own way from there. It was up a flight of stairs – or, more precisely, a swooping soar of stairs that led to an eyrie. Not only did the office seem to hang precariously out over the main room, but the main walls were all glass, without even a rail for reassurance. Mitch had to think it must leave the occupant feeling a little vulnerable.

Which perhaps at least partly explained the fact that everything in the office seemed tightly reined in and under control – including the editor, Eva Lewis. Mitch lingered by the open door for a long moment, watching her while she worked intently at her computer, a lit cigarette hanging from her lips. Mitch was certain that the No Smoking rules were as ubiquitous here as in the States, so he had to admire her for that. She seemed the antithesis of her cousin Tom in other ways as well: she was too thin, and her face was pale and drawn. There was a good chance that she had beautiful long red hair and plenty of it, but it was pulled back so tightly into a bun that Mitch couldn't be sure. He wondered if that was the color Tom's hair had been before the sun and salt had bleached it.

Mitch was thinking far too much about Tom Lewis, obviously. He knocked on Eva's door, and walked in. "Hi. I'm, uh – I'm Martin Delmonaco."

Eva stared up at him, and her lips thinned as she took a drag on her smoke, but otherwise she remained blank.

"Your cousin Tom sent me … ? I'm gonna be working for both of you."

Realization finally dawned. Eva stood, and leaned across the desk to shake hands. "Tom didn't tell me what name you'd be using, Mr. Rebecki.

You said Martin Delmonaco? That's fine." She straightened up again, and coolly considered him for a moment before adding, "No one else knows about this."

Mitch pulled out his own cigarettes and lit one, though he knew he shouldn't. He hated being here, but Eva didn't deserve to bear the brunt of his resentment. Rather the opposite, of course. Mitch managed to say, "Thanks. I appreciate it."

She barely even reacted to that with a lift of her chin. "Tom said you're good but you need to keep your head down. There's an election soon in one of the local councils, so I'll have you cover that. Nothing too controversial there, and I doubt the results are going to surprise anyone. I'll take you down to your desk."

Mitch followed her out of her office and down the swoop of stairs to the main room. A local council. He could hardly contain his excitement.

"You can work from here for Tom's lifestyle pieces, too," Eva was continuing over her shoulder as they crossed the room. "Use whatever facilities you need."

They reached a spare desk. It was tucked away in the furthest corner of the floor, but the noise and bustle seemed barely an arm's length away. Mitch wasn't impressed. He'd had his own office for years back home … Not that anything about this whole stupid situation was Eva's fault, he reminded himself. "Uh, thanks. You're being very generous."

She nodded this time. There was a pause while Eva lit another cigarette. Mitch took a covert look around, and noted that nobody else in the office but Mitch and Eva were smoking. He stubbed out his own smoke in the trash, and forced himself not to light another.

Eva seemed to run on never-unwinding nervous energy, but after she took a long drag she stepped marginally closer and stilled for a moment. "Tom's been a friend to me," she quietly confided. "I worked in your L.A. bureau for a while, before getting this job."

O.K., that sparked a modicum of interest. Mitch was just about to open his mouth to push her for more information, when Eva caught sight of somebody, and turned away.

"Cody!" Apparently Eva was calling to a young woman who was talking with one of the reporters at his desk, showing him a series of printed photos. "Cody!"

The young woman finally heard her, and straightened up. She took a moment to sift through the photos for one in particular, placed it on the journalist's desk with a tap-tap of her forefinger, then headed towards Eva and Mitch. As she walked, her left hand wrapped protectively around the camera hanging from her neck, settling it close against her body as if that's where it fit best.

"Cody," said Eva as she finally drew near. "Come and meet Martin Delmonaco. He's the American journalist who'll be doing those lifestyle pieces I told you about. Mr. Delmonaco, this is Jane Cody, one of our best photographers."

The young woman leaned in to shake hands. "Call me Cody," she said to Mitch, with a grin that most people would surely find infectious. She had short dark hair sticking up every which way, as if she had too much energy to be contained.

"Hi. I'm Mit- Martin."

She laughed good-naturedly at his apparent stutter, and Mitch joined in, a little chagrined. "Jet-lag's a bitch," said Cody.

"You're not wrong."

Eva had already taken a step or two away, obviously uninterested in socializing. She took a long drag, looking as if her thoughts were already elsewhere, before she turned back again. "Cody, take whatever shots Mr. Delmonaco needs – and don't embarrass us, these are going in the *New York Times*. As for the local stories, Mr. Delmonaco – Martin – the library sent up some reading material for you, including the council's latest annual report. I'm sure you can quickly get up to speed."

So the pile of stuff on his new desk wasn't just random detritus. Martin heaved a sigh when he saw there was not just one but three annual reports awaiting him.

"Cody," Eva was continuing as she started to walk off, "show Martin the facilities here, and take him to H.R., alright?"

"Sure," said Cody.

"Wait!" cried Mitch. When Eva turned around, he said, "Actually, I've got to see about renting somewhere, the hotel's gonna blow my budget. Any chance of putting this off till tomorrow?"

Eva glared at him, perhaps just for appearance's sake, then relented. "Let Cody show you around here first, then take the rest of the day off. I'll see you bright and early tomorrow."

"Thanks." And he muttered to himself, "You'll see me early, anyway …"

Catching this, Cody laughed loudly enough to earn a parting glare from Eva. Cody snapped a picture of her stalking away, and then took one of Mitch gazing down at his desk with an irritable scowl.

"Come on, then," Cody said to him. "I'll show you who's what, what's where, and if you're very lucky, where's who."

Cody made for mildly amusing company and the time Mitch spent with her flew by quite quickly – even the hour they spent in Human Resources. Or maybe it was just the effect of jet-lag, with time dragging or fleeting, or zooming from one speed to the other and back again like a bad hallucinogenic trip.

The best part was that she didn't pass any smart remarks when Mitch began to make his excuses, but instead simply escorted him back down to the front lobby of the building. "Thanks," said Mitch.

"No worries," she replied. "So, I'll see you tomorrow, right?"

"Right." Mitch turned away, left his temporary pass on the reception desk, and headed for the doors.

"Mr. Delmonaco!"

The sun was beyond bright out there. While the building was full of light, it was nothing like the glare Mitch could see through the glass frontage. He shuddered a little, feeling that headache gather itself for the attack.

"Mr. Delmonaco!"

"Hey, Martin!" Cody called, and came jogging over to him.

Mitch belatedly turned, and found the security guard on his feet behind the desk, and Cody approaching with an envelope in her hand. "Oh," he said like an idiot, and made a futile gesture indicating something like, well, his head would have been in the clouds if there actually were any.

The guard replied with a 'not a problem' gesture, and turned his attention to other things.

"What's this?" Mitch asked, taking the envelope without much enthusiasm. "Not another form to fill in?"

"Dunno," Cody replied, "but that's Eva's handwriting."

Mitch frowned at his name – his fake name – on the envelope, and then turned it over to tear it open. A moment later his brow lifted in astonishment. It was a letter addressed 'To Whom It May Concern', and provided a character reference ending with an endorsement of him as a trustworthy and reliable – and financially solvent – tenant. "Oh," he said again.

"Alright? Whatever it is?" Cody was making a point of not peering at the letter though she was obviously itching with curiosity.

Mitch handed it to her to read. "It's just that I wasn't expecting –" he began.

But Cody just nodded. "Don't let the brusque manner fool you," she advised. "Eva really is brusque. But every now and then she can be incredibly thoughtful."

"Yeah." Mitch took back the letter and pocketed it, and nodded a farewell. "Tomorrow, then."

Cody nodded, too. "See ya!"

Mitch didn't exactly have high expectations for his temporary home. He also discovered that his budget was more than adequate to cover the costs of living in Sydney; the locals apparently thought rental prices were extortionate, but then they weren't New Yorkers. So Mitch made for an undemanding client, and a real estate agent had him sorted out within a couple of hours.

That afternoon, Mitch found himself and his suitcases standing outside a Victorian-era terrace house in Balmain, staring up at it and wondering if he was the only person immune to what the agent had insisted was 'charm'. It was certainly a little more flamboyant than his Manhattan apartment, with its flaking soft yellow paint and cast iron railings, but that meant pretty much nada to Mitch.

He took down the agency's For Rent sign, and then, having nowhere to put the thing, dumped it on the uneven paving stones in the tiny front courtyard. Then he wheeled his suitcases up the little path. As he tried to fit the unfamiliar key in the lock of the front door, he was startled by somebody greeting him.

"Good afternoon, sir."

Mitch spun around to find two uniformed cops on the sidewalk where he himself had been standing moments before. He grimaced a little, having had quite enough of police officers lately. "Uh, yeah, hi."

The one who'd spoken was a young woman and the other an older man. Mitch had no idea how the whole Australian melting pot worked, but if he had to guess he'd say *she* was of Japanese descent and *he* was mostly Irish. In fact, the man's skin was so pasty Mitch wondered how he managed not to get burnt in the notoriously harsh Australian sun. Both had pleasant, relaxed demeanors – though why wouldn't they, when their duties involved little more than sauntering down suburban streets … ?

"Thought we'd introduce ourselves," the woman continued. "I'm Constable Adena Nakano, this is Constable Jack Wethers, and this is our beat." She tipped her chin towards the terrace house. "You must have just rented this place."

"Yeah."

Nakano smiled, unfazed by his unwillingness to cooperate in the conversation. "It's a nice place, it's never on the market for long. I hope you like living here. And if there's anything we can help you with, just ask."

"Sure," he said. Mitch walked back down the path to take the business card she proffered. Then he turned away, and so did she. Except –

"Sunscreen," said Wethers.

"What?" said Mitch. He glanced at Nakano, but she just smiled.

"Sunscreen." Wethers leaned in a little as if sharing a confidence. "You were wondering how I deal with my pale skin in this climate. Lots and lots of sunscreen lotion."

Mitch shook his head, and managed to say, "Good to know."

Nakano turned to go, and Wethers followed after her with a wave back at Mitch. "Don't forget to Slip-Slop-Slap, sir!"

The two of them headed up the street, followed for a moment by Mitch's sour gaze. Then he returned to wrestling with the front door lock.

Three

Meaningless or not, Mitch wasn't going to shirk the work.

On a sunny day that most of the locals seemed to think enchanting, Mitch found himself standing beside Cody on one side of a busy suburban street lined with shops, staring across at a free sausage sizzle on the opposite sidewalk. The stall itself and most of the nearby surfaces were covered with election posters. One of the candidates for the council was there, shaking hands with the shoppers and passers-by, talking with them if he got the chance, though of course most of them were just interested in the free food. Mitch couldn't deny the delights of the smell of frying onion, but otherwise he felt little more than dumbfounded.

"This is *it*?" Mitch eventually demanded. "This is what you charmingly call electioneering in this country?"

"It's not like it's a federal election," Cody replied, sounding more reasonable and amused than defensive.

"Oh, they'd go the full barbecue for that? I can't believe it – I'm covering a sausage sizzle …"

Cody took a couple of shots of the electioneering action, such as it was, with her ever-present camera. Then she turned the camera towards Mitch and stared at him through the lens. "Pride comes before a fall, huh, Marty?"

He gave a half-shrug, irritably adjusting the strap of his laptop bag on the other shoulder. She took the shot at just the right – wrong – moment. "I've fallen already," Mitch muttered. He lit up a cigarette.

Cody took another shot just as he lowered his hands, which would probably make him look like he was hanging his head.

"God, where are the election issues?" Mitch burst out with a sweeping gesture. "The controversies? The embarrassing skeletons in the candidates' closets?"

"There are issues," she replied, still not taking umbrage. "Water quality at the beach. Low-rent housing projects. A pedestrian crossing on Marsden Street. Discounts on council rates for seniors. That kind of thing."

Mitch grimaced and turned away. Almost without thinking, he dug his hand into his pocket and pulled out his cell phone. He checked for new messages, but of course there weren't any. He was a long way from home, and the difference in time zones wouldn't help.

"Come on," Mitch said, heading off down the street. "This is ridiculous. There's nothing for us here."

Cody's car was a bright blue Toyota RAV4, a mini S.U.V., that Mitch thought a bit ridiculous for city driving, but somehow it was very Australian. Very Cody. Very much what she would term 'fun'. It was also very convenient, so he resigned himself to being seen in it … Not that anybody of any importance was going to witness this indignity, so really what did it even matter? Mitch sighed.

"So," said Cody, casting him a glance, "you wanna tell me why I get to be your chauffeur as well as your photographer … ?"

"I don't drive," he replied.

She turned to stare at him for an unnervingly long moment, and then exclaimed in disbelief, "You can't drive?!"

"Pay attention," he grumbled, meaning to the road as well as the specifics of their conversation. "I didn't say I can't drive. I said I *don't*."

She looked at him doubtingly.

"New Yorkers don't drive. It's years since I have." After a moment, Mitch added, "I left all that behind."

"You won't have forgotten how … It's like riding a bicycle!" Cody let a beat go by, and then burst into delighted laughter at the inappropriate simile. When Mitch couldn't quite resist a smile, Cody added insult to injury by mixing metaphors. "You wanna get back on that horse? You can have a go at driving this, if you want."

He let his smile increase a little in gratitude, but said, "Nah … I let my license lapse, and there's your insurance to think of – and in any case, you all drive on the wrong side of the road. Next question?"

She glanced a grin at him before saying, "O.K., well, what are we doing for the first lifestyle article? What do you need from me?"

"Just get me some standard shots of the Bridge, the Harbor, the Opera House, all that stuff. I'm doing the *Everybody's Favorite Tourist Destination* thing."

"Ho hum."

"Yeah, you've probably got stock shots on file already."

Cody sighed. "I guess at least you can't go wrong featuring the harbor, anyway. It's beautiful."

"That's beautiful? Ever heard of San Francisco?"

"Hey, I've *been* there. San Francisco Bay is cold, man. It's awesome, but it's not beautiful."

Mitch huffed, and didn't bother replying. Even Cody was looking slightly disgruntled at this point. They continued on in silence.

Mitch soon settled into a routine. Each morning, early, he would drag himself out of bed and into a gray sweat suit, and go for a jog down along the waterfront. On his way back he'd drop in at the local stores to pick up his order of newspapers. He rather liked that quiet hour while the air was crisp and the day was still fresh. There would be a few people around, but not many, and they all respected his solitude. Once Mitch became a familiar sight, a couple of the regulars would nod a greeting to which he responded in kind, but nothing was permitted to disturb the peace.

One morning, as Mitch attempted once more to unlock his front door – something he still didn't have the knack of – he noticed a stray cat had ventured into the little courtyard, apparently looking for food. Maybe even affection. It wouldn't have much luck, of course, being black. People were still superstitious about black cats being bad luck. Absolute nonsense, obviously – but then again, the cat wasn't going to have any better luck with Mitch.

He stared at the thing for a long moment. Then he turned away, and headed inside.

Breakfast consisted of a mug of coffee and a cigarette. He consumed both while spreading the newspapers across the table and poring over them. The papers were always American, of course, and he always began with the *New York Times*. Every now and then he'd find a story relating to Cicioni, or mention of him in some other piece. That particular morning, he discovered a story with the headline *Cicioni Donation to School Library*, which made him snort with skeptical amusement. Well, the piece wasn't exactly relevant let alone significant, but he cut it out anyway, and carefully slipped it into a folder along with the few others he'd collected.

Mitch sighed, lit up another smoke, and continued his search.

While Mitch was drinking coffee and tracking Cicioni through the *New York Times*, Cody was wolfing down a large bowl of muesli with sliced banana and searching through the latest issue of *Who Weekly* magazine.

Cody lived in an apartment on the top floor of a tower block. It was a modest place, but she'd adapted it to suit her priorities, and it fit her well. The main living room, where she was sitting now, had the walls and ceiling painted white with the bare floorboards whitewashed. A large window and a huge skylight ensured the room glowed with natural light. Her photography equipment had pride of place, while the few mundane necessities of life – a small table and two chairs, a sofa, a TV – were low in stature and pushed against the edges of the space.

She was currently sitting at the table, with one leg curled under her and the other occasionally kicking along with an unheard beat. After some browsing of *Who Weekly*, Cody at last discovered what she'd been hoping for, and with a delighted grin carefully clipped out a photo from the *Star Tracks* pages. The subject of the picture was Rory Pierce, a beautiful man in his early thirties, with long dark-gold hair and an arresting grin. He was dressed in expensive-looking casual gear, and had apparently been attending a cinema on George Street.

The one indulgence, the one splash of color in the room, was a portion of wall already overflowing with images of the same man. Cody took the photo over there and found a place to pin it where it wouldn't obscure any of her particular favorites. After ogling her latest acquisition Cody spent some time revisiting the other photos, her breakfast forgotten. In some of the images Rory was in offices or restaurants dressed in trendy business suits, in others he was on a beach in a t-shirt and board-shorts. In all of them, he looked happy and relaxed with a range of effortless smiles. In all of them, he was very easy on the eye. In some, he was a visual feast.

Eventually, though, Cody's phone buzzed – and when she checked her watch for the time, she muttered a curse. One last glance at the images of Rory, and she quickly grabbed up her bag and camera, before dashing for the front door.

About the time Cody was due to pick him up, Mitch stepped out his front door. He paused for a moment to lock it – a task always easier than unlocking it, for some unfathomable reason – and then headed down the path to wait on the sidewalk. There was no sign yet of the bright blue RAV4, but that wasn't unexpected. The traffic was forever variable, as was Cody's sense of punctuality.

As luck would have it, the two local cops, Adena Nakano and Jack Wethers, chose those few minutes in which to walk by on their regular beat. They both smiled and nodded a greeting to Mitch, who responded ungraciously. But what the hell could they expect at this time of the morning, when he was still relatively uncaffeinated?

At last Cody pulled up in her RAV4, and Mitch climbed into the passenger seat which was of course on the wrong side of the car. Whenever Mitch thought he'd regained his equilibrium, something as insignificant as that would disorient him all over again. Cody didn't help matters, as she lifted her camera from its usual place slung around her neck and took a shot of Mitch scowling.

"For God's sake! Don't you ever put that thing away?" Mitch batted at the camera, only half in jest, and she shielded it within the circle of her arms. Cody would probably risk life and limb to protect that damned camera.

A moment later the RAV4 sped away, tearing past Nakano and Wethers, and not stopping at the stop sign on the corner. "*I totally paused!*" cried Cody, as she always did, before bursting into laughter, also not unexpected.

Mitch sighed and shook his head. "It's way too early," he grumbled. But he couldn't help noticing that he seemed to be smiling. Just a little.

One of Cody's better qualities was that she was always ready for a good-natured argument. There were times, however, when her combative spirit went to waste because the two of them weren't only not on the same page but not even in the same book.

Mitch had made the mistake of asking if Cody had been quoting something, and for his troubles received a long diatribe about the validity of modern adaptations of classic novels. Apparently Cody was arguing in support of the notion, though most of it was lost on Mitch. The film she was using as an example was apparently titled *Clueless*, which in itself undermined her case. Not that Mitch pointed that out; he was too enervated that morning to want the bother of being cogent. Finally Cody reached a triumphant conclusion just as they entered the front lobby at work. She looked at him with bright dark eyes, waiting on his reaction.

"I don't have an opinion," Mitch said with a shrug. "I don't even read novels."

"What?!" She stalled physically and verbally for a long moment, before protesting, "Why d'you let me rattle on?"

"You seemed to be enjoying yourself."

"Right … Well …" Then an idea occurred to her. "I'm gonna work out a novel to recommend to you. I'm gonna find one you'll love, and then there'll be no stopping you."

"There's no need. Real life has its own stories. There's always plenty going on, if you look carefully enough."

Cody narrowed her eyes at him. "Even here in Oz?"

He grinned. "Touché. Alright," he added, leading the way towards the security barriers through which they needed to pass. "Find me one, and I'll give it a try."

"*It is only a novel …*" Cody opined as she waved farewell and headed in the direction of her own office. "*Only some work in which the greatest powers of the mind are displayed, in which the most thorough knowledge of human nature –*"

Mitch didn't hear any more of what must be another quote. He made for the newsroom, and threaded through the cubicles to his desk. He passed Eva, who was smoking as usual and laying down the law to a couple of the other reporters. She hardly even glanced at Mitch, which naturally was fine by him.

Once he was settled at his desk, he cast a morose gaze upon the barely disturbed reading material about the local council, and he sighed heavily.

He was just about to reach a hand towards the latest annual report when the land-line rang, startling him out of his stupor. He picked up the handset instead. "Yeah?"

A formal though vaguely familiar voice asked, "May I speak to Martin Delmonaco, please?"

"That's me."

"Good morning, Mr. Delmonaco, this is James Toller from Immigration. You might remember that I asked you to advise us of your residential address once you'd settled."

Mitch rolled his eyes, and pondered explaining that he'd had more important things on his mind. He quickly concluded, however, that would just waste even more time. "Sure," he replied in tones that might pass as friendly. "I'm at 523 Gabriel Street, Balmain."

The rattle of keystrokes as this was typed into a computer. "And the postcode, sir?"

"No idea," he cheerfully replied.

Toller didn't even let a beat go by. "Thank you, Mr. Delmonaco. I appreciate your cooperation."

"Yeah, sure. Whatever." And he hung up, abruptly feeling unamused. In fact, he felt thoroughly stultified. Mitch dropped his head to the desk, wondering yet again at where he found himself.

The phone rang again, and he grabbed at it irritably. "Yeah, and what now?"

But it wasn't James Toller's polite Zen tones that responded. It was Tom Lewis, in full-blown blistering anger. "What the hell is this crap you're sending me, Mitch?"

"Tom!" Mitch found himself exclaiming. Hearing his editor was like being thrown a lifeline when he was drowning.

It was early evening for Tom in New York, and the newsroom was starting to winnow down to the stalwarts. Nevertheless, he'd closed the door to his office before making the call. He was sitting at his desk glaring down at a printed proof copy of the Sunday supplement, open to the first of two double-page spreads of Mitch's article. "*Sydney: Everybody's Favorite Tourist Destination*, my arse," he complained. "It's boring."

"You're telling me," Mitch replied fervently. "I'm coming back home to New York, Tom, I don't care what you say. I wanna return to civilization!"

Tom rolled his eyes, and clarified, "The *article* is boring! Even I can't see how to save it, and I'm a damn good editor. The photos are good, but you can do better than this, Mitch."

"Yeah, I can do *real* stories …"

"Then get over yourself, and *do* one!" Tom thundered. "If you can't take this seriously then I don't want you back."

This time it was Tom who hung up abruptly. He glared at the article for another long moment – and then he dumped the proof in the trash. When he picked up the phone again, it was to call Gail, who edited the supplement.

Mitch was left staring at the phone in mild shock. He slowly put the handset down, and sat back. A *real* story … about *Sydney* … What could he *possibly* … ?

But then Mitch had an idea. It was such a good and provoking idea that it almost betrayed him into a wicked smile. He got up, and strode out of the main room, heading for Cody's office.

Just as in Cody's living room, she had one wall of her office covered in photos. In this case, however, they were all photos that she had taken. There were large cityscapes and unexpected macros, there were thoughtfully composed pieces and hastily-caught moments. There were portraits both formal and informal, there were abundant examples of street photography – and scattered through these were shots taken from afar of the beautiful, the intriguing Rory Pierce.

Despite the potential distraction, however, she was working when Martin burst in – she was on the computer cropping and resizing what she thought were her best three shots of the Lord Mayor laying the foundation stone for a new courthouse.

"I've got an idea for my next story," Martin declared, suddenly pushing in through the doorway.

To say Cody was startled would be an understatement; hardly anyone visited her in her solitary basement lair. "For the *Times*? What's that, then?" she asked as she typed the relevant journalist's name and then Eva's name into the address box in an email.

"I'll tell you on the way. Come on!"

Cody groaned a little, and typed 'Take your pick!' into the subject line, before dragging the three photos into the message body.

"It's not boring," Martin continued. "I can promise you that."

"Alright, alright," she grumbled, hitting the Send button.

Martin was already gone. Cody groaned again, grabbed up her camera and her keys, and dashed out after him.

Soon Mitch and Cody were on Oxford Street, just outside the city center in Darlinghurst, sitting at a café table that was loaded down with her camera, his laptop, their cell phones, and two espressos. The latter were apparently known as 'short blacks' in Australia, a rather undignified name that Mitch couldn't see himself ever using. His bemusement about the coffee had made Cody chuckle – but his idea for a story had made her laugh out loud. Even Mitch was feeling mildly amused.

And she'd obviously brought him to the right place. A mainstream customer might not pick up on the fact that the colorful mix of crockery made a rainbow, the artistic photos of beach lifeguards on the walls provided a perfect subject for the gay male gaze, and the waiter was dressed to match Jean Paul Gaultier's 'Le Male' cologne bottle … but Mitch felt comfortable there. The place was subtle but unashamed. Maybe there were some things that Australians weren't so bad at, after all.

Cody downed half her espresso in a gulp, and laughed again. "*Sydney's Thriving Gay and Lesbian Community* … God, Martin, that'll be priceless!"

"Thanks," he said, letting his mouth quirk into a brief smile, then taking a sip of coffee to cover it.

"But," she continued, "is that really what New Yorkers wanna read over their croissants and lattés on a Sunday morning?"

"That's bagels and macchiatos, thank you." Mitch shrugged. "Anyway, who cares? If Tom wants an interesting article, I can give him plenty of color and controversy."

"Hey, I've got some great photos from the last Mardi Gras you can use. And you can do a whole lot of research right here on Oxford Street. There's an independent bookshop just a few doors up; that'd make a great place to start. Oh, and when you're done here, we can do King Street in Newtown."

"What's in Newtown?"

Cody lit up in rather overdone excitement. "That's where you'll be dipping me in honey and throwing me to the lesbians."

"Uh huh," Mitch replied skeptically. He was pretty sure Cody was straight, but maybe she'd measure a one on the Kinsey scale. Mitch himself was a six, no doubt about it.

"Please," said Cody.

"Yeah, and don't you think they'll be throwing you right back, if I do?" Mitch sat up in his chair, took another sip of espresso, and opened up his laptop. They were sitting outside, so while the computer was booting up he lit a cigarette. And he studiously avoided meeting Cody's searching gaze.

Eventually, however, she declared, "Marty, I do believe you're smiling! No … Yes … Oh yes, there it is again!" And she turned her camera on him, about to record this historic moment.

Mitch scowled at her. "Why d'you keep doing that?" he asked irritably. "You can't see your whole life through a lens."

"Right … You can talk," she responded, gesturing at his laptop. "You see everything through the words on your screen."

"It's not the same. It's not my Siamese twin."

"It's my *job* to be prepared for –"

Mitch gave her a sardonic look, and Cody's protest faltered into silence.

They finished their espressos in mutual annoyance. Mitch slumped in his chair and stared off into the Oxford Street traffic, ignoring his laptop after all – not that he was deigning to accept her point. Cody had carefully put her camera down on the table, though she didn't pack it away.

For some unfathomable reason, however, during those few minutes Cody's mood slid from aggrieved back to amused. It was as if she'd realized she was in on some kind of secret. By the time she had counted out enough change to cover her coffee, and gathered her things together, she was smiling secretively. "Gotta run, Marty," she said, standing up from the table.

"Already?" He scowled again, and reached a hand to close the laptop.

"Nah, you stay here and do some research, yeah? Have fun!"

"What?"

"Um … Go browse the bookshop if nothing else beckons. Then you catch a cab back, and charge it to expenses. O.K.?"

"Oh God," he grumbled. "O.K. If I must."

"I'll see ya in the morning, as usual."

Mitch lifted his chin in reluctant acknowledgement, and let her go without further protest. He sighed, glanced around for the waiter – who was currently otherwise occupied – and sat up to log in to his computer. He could at least start making some notes, and if the café had Wi-Fi then he could do some searching, get some back-story, while catering to his caffeine needs.

Eventually the waiter must have sensed he was wanted, and came over to stand by Mitch's table. "At last!" Mitch said, though without much heat. When he looked up, though, he discovered that it wasn't the waiter. "Oh."

The warm dark gaze was familiar, as was the amused and slightly suggestive smile. It only took a moment for Mitch to recall the rather different context in which they'd met before. In which they'd had … a horribly intimate encounter.

"It's you!" Mitch blurted, losing his last shred of street cred.

"Yes, sir."

It was the Customs Officer, of course, looking even more attractive in his civilian clothes of blue jeans, a white t-shirt, and a green shirt worn loose over the top. Just to add to the enticements he carried a well-loved paperback in one hand, with the corner of a bookmark poking out at an angle as if hastily placed. Mitch made a mental note to find out the title and author. Then he scrambled to remember the guy's name. "It's Samuel Windrayne, right?"

"Yes, sir. You can call me Sam, if you want." After a moment, he asked, "Can I buy you a drink, sir?"

Mitch considered him carefully. His use of the term 'sir' must surely be ironic, even if the offer and the implied intent was sincere. He was polite, but not deferential. He really was very enticing, and could surely have his choice of men. Mitch knew that he himself wasn't handsome, and he'd never try to pretend otherwise, but he made an effort and he was presentable enough. He got his share of attention when he sought it. But he never would have expected …

Mitch took a breath, and pointed out, "You've already seen all there is to see."

"Yes, sir. And I'd like to buy you a drink."

Well. How was he supposed to resist this gentle persistence? "O.K. Sure." Mitch indicated the chair that Cody had vacated, and then looked up to find that the waiter was hovering, awaiting their order with a look of smug satisfaction. Mitch smiled to himself wryly, and ordered another espresso. If his companion had expected Mitch to take advantage of the café's liquor license, he didn't miss a beat; he ordered a latté.

Mitch didn't know whether to be surprised or not, afterwards, to realize they hadn't once talked about books.

Cody was already waiting by the time Mitch finally rushed out his front door the next morning. She'd been there so long she'd even switched off the ignition of her RAV4, instead of leaving it idling as she usually did. She didn't seem surprised, however, by his tardiness, and she broke into a grin as soon as she saw him.

Mitch himself couldn't help betraying his own sense of satisfaction, despite feeling a bit worse for wear. He tried to quell his smile, but it just wouldn't die. As a result Cody let out a laugh and a whoop as he climbed into the car. Mitch couldn't even find it in himself to protest when she turned her camera on him and took a photo.

"Oh my God, you *are* in a good mood!" she declared.

"Could be," Mitch allowed. He hadn't quit smiling yet, despite his best efforts.

"So, how did the *research* go last night … ? That's an 'I got lucky' smile, right?" She crowed when he didn't deny the matter. "I knew it! Well, it was either gonna be that or a 'some dumb fag hit on me' frown …"

Mitch did almost manage a frown at her then. There was only so much exuberance he could take first thing in the morning. "Settle down, would you? I'm the one who got lucky, O.K.? Not you."

"Did you *interview* him … ?"

Mitch rolled his eyes. "For God's sake, Cody, back off, will you? Let's get to work."

"Alright, alright," she mock-grumbled. Then she grinned at him again. "Way to go, though, Marty. I'm proud of you."

"Just drive!"

At last Cody started the car and pulled away from the curb, failing to signal but letting out another whoop.

Neither Cody nor Mitch noticed that Constables Nakano and Wethers were walking up the sidewalk. The two cops paused to watch the RAV4 speed off down the street, and then exchanged a rueful glance. "Next time," said Wethers as they turned to continue on their way.

"What are you going to do?" asked Nakano. "Run after her to issue a caution?"

"Something like that," he agreed equably.

Nakano lifted her chin in acknowledgement of the humor, and then asked in less ironic tones, "Remember I took that call from Immigration yesterday?"

"Yeah."

"They want us to keep an eye on him."

"Seriously?"

"Seriously. Martin Delmonaco, U.S. citizen, lives at 523 Gabriel. Apparently he's not quite what he seems to be."

Wethers turned for a moment to gaze towards where Mitch, Cody and the RAV4 had disappeared into the Sydney traffic. Then he turned back to look at Nakano. "So what do they think he is?"

"They don't know … and I don't know, either." She cast her partner a troubled glance. "But maybe I was wrong about him. Maybe he's one of the bad guys."

Wethers just nodded thoughtfully.

As promised – or was that threatened? – Cody took Mitch to Newtown one day, and drove him down King Street, chattering away as usual and pointing out the sights, such as they were. It all looked rather suburban to Mitch, with low-rise buildings, and store-fronts that didn't extend higher than the awnings or overhangs. Still, he could see that there was some color there, and an interesting balance between comfortably shabby and what passed as trendy in Sydney.

"I guess we can amp up the 'character' angle," he remarked. Glancing down the side streets he glimpsed modest modern apartment blocks as well as the ubiquitous Victorian-era terrace houses with cast iron railings on their fences and balconies. "Is this typical Sydney suburbia, or are you going to tell me it's all Lesbian Chic?"

Cody widened her eyes at him in exaggerated disbelief. "I'm not even going to dignify that," she said. "Oh man, you just wait until December when the frangipani trees start to bloom." Cody waved a hand to indicate one of the many compact, bare trees that lined the streets. "Even *you're* gonna agree this place is beautiful."

"Uh huh," he responded in flat ironic tones.

Soon, however, Mitch was established contentedly enough at a table outside a café, letting the relaxed atmosphere of the place drift past him, while he smoked and tapped away at his laptop. He had the latest issues of *Out in Sydney*, *Outrage* and *Sydney Star Observer* spread across the table for the purposes of research, and one of the staff was currently brewing his third 'short black'.

Cody, meanwhile, seemed to be in her element, ambushing passers-by and asking to take their photo in the spring sunshine. A lesbian couple happily posed for her with their arms around each other, and then a gay couple posed holding hands. Individuals composed themselves with smiles that ranged from cheerful to thoughtful to enigmatic. Nobody seemed overly uncomfortable in being 'out', though Mitch guessed they might have made a point of avoiding King Street if they were – or at least of avoiding Cody.

After a while Mitch and Cody switched venue to a pub, which seemed to date back some decades, perhaps almost a century. The green tiles, gold-painted walls and time-polished wood glowed in the late afternoon sunlight pouring through the windows. Even Mitch could have taken a half-decent shot or two with such visuals. Instead he sat back and watched as Cody chatted with a group of women playing pool, soon gaining their trust. Unlike the clientele at the café, the pub's customers seemed to be more working class, even manual laborers. They wore checked flannel shirts open over dark-blue vests, with grubby canvas pants and scuffed working boots. They were rough and honest and occasionally very funny, and Cody's photos brought out their steadfast, forthright but not humorless nature.

The evening began drawing in. The streetlights and store-fronts flickered into bright life, turning the sky a dark blue. The slight chill in the air intensified, and the bustle of people grew as they headed home from work or came to King Street for the evening.

Mitch found himself in a late-opening bookstore, interviewing the staff and the customers. Cody took a few photos but then started browsing the shelves. There was the usual mix of local and international gay newspapers and magazines, all kinds of books, raunchy gifts and greeting cards and calendars … Even Cody occasionally looked shocked at what she found.

Night fell, and the chill in the air developed a bite. Mitch had to force himself to remember that it actually was spring here on this side of the globe, and not fall. It was oddly disorienting even for an urban creature like Mitch, when the days were about the same length as back home, and the temperature was much the same, but the leaves were budding green rather than turning gold.

Mitch had scored an invitation to a regular monthly meeting of a local gay rights group, so he spent a couple of hours watching and listening while the committee of gay men and lesbians debated funding and activism. It was interesting enough, even if all the issues were small scale and parochial – though Cody soon nodded off, and Mitch himself felt dazed and weary by the end.

Cody livened up again once they were at a nightclub. Within moments she had joined the mass of humanity out on the dance floor and was grooving to the beat. Even then she still had her camera strap slung round her neck, and she held the camera safe in one hand, almost as if she were dancing with it. Mitch watched her for long moments, amused, before he turned away and headed for the bar.

He ended up standing next to a guy who looked not only pleasant but moderately intelligent, and Mitch tried to strike up a conversation. They were thwarted by the continuing thump-throb of loud music, so there was no question of an interview or a verbal negotiation. When the guy indicated the dance floor with a querying brow, Mitch shook his head. He didn't dance.

So, of course, soon the guy was snagged by somebody with a bit more initiative – though Mitch was thrown the consolation of a regretful glance. Instead of pursuing other options, Mitch settled in and watched Cody. It seemed she was lost in the music and the moves, all her cares and concerns and self-consciousness blasted away. In those moments, Mitch could see the attraction of dancing. Absolutely.

The next morning when Mitch walked into Cody's office, he found her still grooving along, though now in silence, with only the memory of the music to drive her. She was gazing at a particular place in her wall of photos, as if lost now in the visuals and what they evoked.

A beat or two later, Cody almost literally jumped to realize she had company. "Marty!" she squeaked. "Honestly …" she protested in something more like her regular voice, turning away with embarrassment splotching her cheeks. "Haven't you heard of knocking?"

"Like you'd have even heard if I had. In any case, the door was open."

Cody was sitting at her desk now, opening folders on her computer and calling up a selection of photos. Mitch took the opportunity of the momentary lull to look at the images on her wall, trying to work out which one she'd been staring at so intently. He thought perhaps it was a photo of a man dressed in an elegant charcoal-gray business suit, with long dark-gold hair and a charmingly wide smile. The man was undeniably gorgeous. Mitch might have even considered dancing with him, too. Not that he would actually dance, either alone or in company. But faced with that guy he'd have thought about it.

"Here," Cody said, calling him over to her computer. "These are all from this year's Mardi Gras. I've got plenty from other years as well, but I figured you'd want the most recent?"

"Sure," he agreed, hauling across her visitor's chair so he could look over her shoulder.

There were a range of photos taken before, during and after the Gay and Lesbian Mardi Gras. Some were posed portrait shots, some were of the parade, others were at the party afterwards, and still more were of the following early morning. All were colorful, vibrant, decadent, in-your-face. Mitch and Cody choose four to submit with the article from which the editor would choose. Mitch loved the poignancy of the shots taken the morning after, most of them in black-and-white, but that wasn't quite the feel he was going for with the article so he left them aside.

Then the two of them went through the photos Cody had taken in Oxford Street and King Street. Again they made a selection of the better ones. Cody added captions to all the ones they'd send, checking her notes for details.

Mitch had the article finished by early that afternoon. It was one of those pieces that just wrote itself, a gift of the Muse directly from her lips to his fingers. He read through it again, just to be sure, and then with a pleased smile attached it to an email along with the zip file of Cody's photographs.

Off it went to New York, where it was too late at night to expect an immediate response. Mitch sat back, and instead of considering his local work, indulged himself in some personal reading. He thought he'd earned it.

The phone on Mitch's desk rang first thing the next morning. If Mitch still had the time difference straight in his head, it must be towards the end of the previous working day in New York. Mitch grinned, and picked up the handset, knowing who it would be. "Yeah?"

Sure enough, Tom's not-so-dulcet tones resounded down the line. "What, are you gonna throw a coming out party, too?"

"Hey, Tom," he greeted the man.

"You've got balls, Mitch."

He grinned harder. "Does that mean you like the article?"

"It's great. It's completely over the top, but it's great." Tom let a beat go by, and then announced, "Gail's running it next week."

There was a slight edginess to his tone that gave Mitch pause. Eventually he concluded, "You telling me she didn't run the last one?"

"It got as far as proofs before I told her to pull it – and you'll thank me for that when you swallow your damn pride. I told her she doesn't owe us any favors. All that piece was good for was curing insomnia."

Mitch was still grinning, almost despite himself. "I can think of better cures."

"Sounds like you're having fun down there, Mitch," Tom observed. "Surprise, surprise."

O.K., that sobered him up, just a little. "No way," Mitch protested, before calling an end to the conversation. "Talk to you next week, right?"

"Right."

Mitch hung up the phone. But his smile lingered, and almost saw him through the entire day.

Four

Reporting on the local council elections did *not* make Mitch smile. It was all so utterly trivial, and there was nothing to be done to transform the stories into anything interesting or amusing.

Today Mitch was in a suburban park witnessing the current mayor launching his urban planning policy, which as far as Mitch could tell contained nothing innovative or even new. If pushed Mitch wouldn't deny that his surroundings were lovely, or that the general mood was up-beat, but he himself was back to being bored and irritable. Even smoking a constant chain of cigarettes didn't cheer him.

He looked around once more, hoping for something to catch his eye. But he didn't care for the election posters, or the streamers and balloons, and he'd already leached what interest he could from the displays of maps and building plans. There was a small crowd of very ordinary people behaving so well that the two security guards present and the few cops weren't called on to do anything more than loiter.

One of the cops, however, eventually made her way over to Mitch in between speeches. "Hello," she said with a sociable smile. "Nice day to be out and about."

Mitch recognized her, but couldn't for the life of him remember her name. He was usually far more attentive than that. Details mattered in his line of work … Well, they mattered back in New York City, anyway. "Yeah, hi," Mitch responded a bit lamely. "Uh, Constable … ?"

"Adena Nakano," she replied, with only the gentlest hint of reproof. "I'm your friendly neighborhood beat cop, remember?"

"Yeah, I remember," he flatly replied. He dropped the butt of his last cigarette and ground it out against the grass, then stuffed his hands into his coat pockets.

Nakano persisted in her interrogation despite Mitch's patent lack of interest in conversing. "You're American, right? The accent is a dead giveaway, of course."

"Not to mention the attitude," he muttered on her behalf, offering a sketchy smile.

"So what brings you to Australia?" she asked, hard on his heels.

"I'm a journalist. Uh … kind of freelance."

"What are you working on? Don't tell me you're fascinated by our local urban planning …"

"I'm absolutely riveted."

She waited for a better answer than that, while he absolutely failed to come up with one. Mitch realized he really must invent a proper cover story about why Martin Delmonaco would want to be on a working holiday in Australia. A story that Mitch could actually inhabit without giving himself away.

"Well," Nakano continued, at last taking pity on him. "I hope you can stay for a while. Sydney is a dream all year round. When do you go home again?"

Mitch shrugged instinctively, looking around at the hoopla. It was already too late with Nakano to pretend to be interested, anyway, so he went with his instincts. "I've got a question for you, Constable Nakano. Cops … ? Security guards? For *this*? What do you think's gonna happen here?"

"Any theories of your own?" she asked.

He huffed. "The worst-case scenario is that somebody's gonna fall asleep during the speech and snore too loudly."

She was amused, but answered with a straight face. "Then the guards can wake him up."

"It's nice that you all take everything here so seriously. But you can't be dealing with the kind of threat that somebody like the mayor of New York City faces every day. This is complete overkill."

After a beat, Nakano said, "I can't tell you why, but today this is justified."

Mitch eyed her for a long moment, suspecting irony. Her serious façade didn't crack, but Mitch remained unconvinced. "Yeah, right," he said, not hesitating to lay on the sarcasm. "Well, you'll excuse me, won't you? I've got an absolutely riveting story to write."

He stalked off towards the mayor, who was finally stepping down from the podium. Mitch was conscious that Nakano was watching him with a puzzled frown on her face … It was only much later – far too late to do anything about it – that he realized she must have been wondering why, if he really was a journalist, Mitch didn't press her for details on why the security that day was justified.

He really wasn't great at this whole undercover thing.

There was a darkroom next to Cody's office, though in these days of digital photography it wasn't used all that often. "There's still something to be said for photographing on film," Cody had announced once. "There's a different quality to it. Almost like … a depth. A hint of that third dimension."

"Digital is more practical for work, though, isn't it?" Mitch had argued. "No real limit to the number of exposures. No processing delays."

"True," she'd agreed with a shrug. "I guess it's more about art." Then she added, "You'd be surprised how many images they want me to print on proper photographic paper, though, rather than run through an ink-jet printer. You can call it snob value, if you want, but they do like to show off the real thing."

That's what Cody was doing on this particular day – printing large black-and-white copies of the newspaper's most recent notable photos. The prints were destined to fill a sequence of frames in the lobby of the executive floor at the top of the building. A fair proportion of the images had been taken by Cody herself, despite the fact she certainly wasn't the only photographer employed by the *Herald*, and the paper routinely sourced photos from freelancers as well.

Mitch was feeling at rather a loss that day, and was disconsolately loitering in the darkroom watching while she worked in the minimal red light. He was fiddling with his pack of cigarettes, because even he drew the line at smoking in such a place. Cody seemed quite content to ignore him, though, unless he spoke.

"O.K.," Mitch eventually said, "so what the hell do I write next? Lifestyle pieces aren't my strength – thank God."

She spared him a glance. "So, what *is* your strength?"

"Never mind," he replied, knowing that it was probably too late to finesse his undercover skills where Cody was concerned. "Where am I supposed to get ideas for topics? This is ridiculous."

There was silence for a while as Cody finished exposing a shot, and slipped the sheet of paper into a chemical bath. An image slowly emerged from what otherwise appeared to be blank paper. Mitch watched along with Cody: it was always quite mesmerizing even if you'd seen it happen a hundred times before. Cody kept an eye on the timer, but also used her own judgment about when to halt the development. This was an image of a man crossing a city street with traffic approaching in the near distance. There was something visually satisfying about the composition, though Mitch had no idea what the news value was.

Cody had just transferred the photograph into the final tray – of water, to wash off the chemicals – when she suddenly lit up with excitement. "Oh my God! Marty! I know what you can do!" She turned to him. "Do a piece on Sydney's architecture! Even you've got to admit it's a beautiful city."

He grimaced a little, but said, "I guess. What's the angle?"

She swished the photograph about in the water for a moment, but then abandoned it to its fate. Instead, she grabbed Mitch's hand and led him into the darkroom's airlock – a tight fit for the two of them, but she didn't seem to care – and then out into her office. The change from the dull red light to the regular fluorescents was disorienting for a moment, but Mitch regained his balance with a couple of blinks and a shake of his head.

Cody walked him to the center of her office floor-space, let go of his hand, and then stood there facing him, staring up at him from only a long-legged pace away.

"There's this architect," Cody said intently. "Rory Pierce. He's incredible, he could take the world by storm. He's the sexiest thing to happen to architecture since … since we lived in caves. You can be his Big International Break."

She went to her wall of photos, and unpinned one of them. It was the photo that Mitch thought she'd been dancing with a couple of days before, the one of the gorgeous man in an elegant suit, with long dark-gold hair and a charming smile. Mitch let his gaze dart over the rest of the wall, and saw the collection included other photos of the same man. Very formally Cody handed the photo over to Mitch, and he took it in both hands.

"This guy's an architect?" Mitch asked. "I saw this photo before. I figured he was an actor or a model."

Cody nodded as if this mistake was perfectly understandable. "Eva can introduce you, get you an exclusive."

That was even more unexpected. "Eva knows him?"

Cody looked somewhat troubled but completely sincere. "They were married for about a year. A friend of mine took the photos at their wedding."

"Eva Lewis?" Mitch clarified, pointing up towards the main newsroom on the floors above.

Another nod from Cody. She glanced about as if to make sure they wouldn't get caught – not that there were ever any other signs of life in this part of the basement – and then went to fetch a presentation folder from the back of a drawer of hanging files. When she brought the folder back to Mitch, he opened it up and then stared at the photo, absolutely stunned.

"That's Eva Lewis … ? Look at her!"

The photo was a head-and-shoulders shot of the bride and groom, with sun-dappled green leaves forming a backdrop. Eva was all joy and radiance, and utterly relaxed. There could hardly be a greater contrast to her current reined-in, under-control perfectionism. Even though her beautiful red hair was put up in a bun it was loosely arranged in the photo, compared to her scraped-back style now.

Eventually Mitch couldn't help noticing, however, that no matter how gorgeous the bride was, the groom was even more so. Rory Pierce was smiling as widely and happily as Eva. In fact, their happiness matched and echoed each other's, as if it were two halves of the one shared emotion. Anybody seeing this photo would assume the couple had every blessing.

"But they only lasted a year?" Mitch asked.

"Yeah …" Cody gusted a sigh. "Can you imagine giving him up? I never did get why she left him."

They both contemplated the photo for a moment more, and then Cody hid it away again.

"So, will you do the article?" she asked as she came back to stand by Mitch.

"On architecture? Sure, I'll think about it …" He wandered off, lifting a hand to Cody in an absentminded farewell, and beginning to turn the matter over in his mind. He was as surprised as anybody else might be that he was indeed thinking about it.

Before Mitch could do another lifestyle piece for Tom, though, he needed to put some time into the local elections. One afternoon Mitch was sitting at a micro-form reader in the *Herald*'s library, looking at old newspaper articles on the council and the mayor, doing background research. It was beyond boring, of course. Everything was so petty and small-scale, and the players didn't even seem aware of that, let alone take the few opportunities to expand.

He found a brief article dated about five years before, about a Hunter Valley vineyard owned by the mayor, and scanned through it for anything of interest. *Mayor Smithson said he was proud of the high quality of wines produced,* the piece mentioned in conclusion, *but declined to comment further.* Mitch frowned. It was inexplicable, really. What kind of businessman refused the chance for free promotion … ?

Still puzzling over that, Mitch glanced through the following couple of pages – and happened to alight on a story about Rory Pierce, whose innovative talent (no doubt augmented by his beauty) was recognized while he was still quite young. Mitch grimaced over the piece and the accompanying grainy black-and-white photo. He wasn't feeling overly inspired but he printed the page anyway, just in case.

The micro-form index led Mitch to another small news article on the mayor's vineyard dated about a year later. Apparently purchases of new land and machinery had been made possible by a new business partner. Details were sketchy, but seemed to involve a silent partner with loads of cash. "How convenient," Mitch muttered.

This did at least set his investigative nose twitching, though chances were it would all come to a whole load of nothing. With some guidance from the librarian – because of course everything here was organized in idiosyncratically Australian ways – Mitch worked through various other records in the library, taking copies along the way to establish the trail of clues. Eventually he discovered that the name of the mayor's business partner was John Bricca. Puzzlingly, Mitch didn't find anything much more than that.

"Have you heard of this guy John Bricca?" Mitch asked the librarian.

She slowly shook her head while glancing through what he'd found and considering the context. Not that she came up with anything. "I don't know the name at all, I'm sorry."

"There's nothing here about other businesses, or family, or anything. So where's the money coming from … ?"

She was as mystified as he was. Which Mitch didn't mind so much, as it meant he might be onto something. Suddenly the local council elections side of his job had become a lot more interesting. Mitch gathered up what he had so far, and headed purposefully out the door.

By the end of the day Mitch still hadn't found anything to confirm or deny his suspicions, so he took the whole thing to Eva. He spread the various copies of things across her desk but she barely glanced at them. Instead she sat back in her chair to listen with one arm across her chest and her legs crossed at the knee, and they both smoked while Mitch paced back and forth, gesticulating his way through the story so far.

When he finally finished talking, he physically paused as well, and looked to her for a reaction.

She took a thoughtful drag on her cigarette, and eventually said, "I don't know the name, either."

At which point, Mitch decided he really must be onto something. "Well, then doesn't that make you wonder? Maybe it's legit, granted – or maybe the mayor is crooked."

Eva didn't seem overly impressed. "Aren't you meant to be staying out of trouble?"

"Oh, come on …" he pleaded in disbelief. "There could be a real story here about corruption. Sure, it's not on the same scale as New York, but this is the kind of thing I was born to write about."

Eva seemed about to say something – and then paused to reconsider while she lit up another cigarette. Apparently she decided to say it anyway. "Tom told me you don't have a life. Not even back home in New York."

"Oh, for God's sake," he muttered.

"Well, I don't have a life, either," Eva continued, "but at least I don't think I was born to be an editor."

"Then I'm one up on you, because at least I have a vocation."

She considered him for a long moment, and then said, "Brett took leave this week – his father died – and Sandy's got the flu. Why don't you write a few film reviews?"

"What the fuck, Eva?" he complained.

"I need you to get over yourself and make a contribution."

Mitch scowled at her. "Yeah, O.K., I'll make a proper contribution, and follow up this story."

Eva remained silent while Mitch gathered up the papers relating to

Bricca and the mayor, and headed for the door.

But Mitch had second thoughts and turned back. "Look," he said, "I'm sure you don't wanna do me any favors right now …"

She rolled her eyes, and prompted, "What d'you need?"

"Can you set me up an exclusive interview with Rory Pierce?"

She didn't react to the name, unless it was to become even colder and more closed off than ever. A tremble of her hand betrayed her, however. Ash fell from her cigarette onto her otherwise pristine desk.

"Why?" she asked.

"I'm thinking of doing a lifestyle piece for the *Times* on Sydney's architecture. Interviewing an architect who actually has some public recognition will add a bit of humanity. Could be a pretty cold subject otherwise."

Throughout that, Eva stared hard ahead of her, out across the newsroom, not moving. Not even taking a drag on her cigarette. Even once Mitch was done, she didn't acknowledge him with so much as a flicker of interest. He let her think it through, though. He had ambushed her, after all.

Eventually Eva stubbed out the remains of her smoke and said, "Alright. There's an official opening on Friday for a new building he designed. I'll get you an invitation."

"Make it two invitations."

Eva looked at him. "Do the lifestyle piece for Tom – but do an article for me as well, on the opening and the building."

"Alright."

"Leave the thing with John Bricca alone. Let someone else run with it."

Mitch nodded, although even Eva must have realized it was more in acknowledgment than agreement. He turned to leave.

But Eva added, "If you're taking Cody, keep an eye on her, alright? Don't let her embarrass herself."

"Hey, don't look to me to babysit!" Mitch protested with an irritable shrug. And he walked out.

The opening on Friday didn't give Mitch much time to prepare, but those sorts of pressures came with the job. He gathered newspaper articles on Pierce and his work, from other sources as well as the *Herald*. Even Mitch had to admit that he became moderately interested when he discovered that this high-flying architect was also involved in developing a low-rent housing project. Although, really, Mitch reflected, and so he should be. Mitch didn't have any time at all for celebrities who didn't 'give back' to the community.

On the Thursday, Mitch walked into Cody's office to find her bursting with excitement. It seemed that she literally couldn't keep still. She got up from her chair and advanced on Mitch as soon as she saw him. "We're still O.K. for the opening tomorrow … ?"

He must have looked a bit startled, because Cody veered off again and paced an aimless circle. "Yeah," said Mitch. "Come and get me about two. If I'm not at my desk, I'll be chasing up stuff on the mayor and his vineyard."

"Two? Make it one-thirty, just in case. Traffic, you know?"

Mitch shook his head, and couldn't help but smile. "Sure, O.K., one-thirty."

Cody's circle had brought her around to confront Mitch again. "Anyway, how the hell can you still be thinking about the boring old mayor when you're about to meet Rory Pierce, the sexiest –"

"Yeah, yeah – the sexiest thing to happen to architecture since the Big Bang. Tell me something, though. The guy's pretty enough, but how can architecture be sexy?"

"*Pretty enough?*" she protested. "What's *wrong* with you? He's gorgeous, he's like some kind of demi-god, and he creates the most beautiful buildings I've ever seen!"

"And that's your objective opinion, is it?"

She mock-growled at his ironic tone. "Anyway, you're researching the wrong sources." She headed back to her desk and pushed a small collection of magazines in Mitch's direction. They were the glossy sort, with titles like *Who* and *Black+White*. Mitch flipped through to the pages Cody had marked with Post-it Notes, to find gushing articles and sumptuous photos devoted more to the man than his work. Still, Rory Pierce did seem to be trying to do something different with his designs, something with flair.

"I guess they are attractive buildings, from what I can see of them. And there's certainly something about him," Mitch found himself adding. "I guess there has to be. How else would an architect get to be a minor celebrity?"

"Minor?! My God, you're blind or blinkered or something. Just wait till tomorrow when you get to see the real thing …"

Mitch snorted a laugh, and headed out again. Though he turned back at the door to ask, "Are you gonna get any sleep tonight?"

"Probably not," Cody cheerfully replied.

"O.K., well, I'll see you bright and early."

"Very bright. Probably very early, too!"

Mitch groaned, and got out of there while the going was good.

Early the next afternoon, Mitch and Cody stood on the sidewalk across the street gazing up at a magnificent new office building. And it was magnificent, even Mitch had to admit that. Even though it appeared to be a regular rectangle, there was something about its shape or its structure, some kind of visual trickery, that made it appear to leap up into the sky.

Cody was awe-struck, of course. And she was trying too hard, all dressed up in bold blues and yellows, as if that would make the difference in Pierce paying her attention. Not that Mitch hadn't put some effort into his own choices … but then again, he always did. He liked wearing smart, good quality clothes. If he had picked out a particularly clever combination of warm grays that morning, it probably didn't have anything to do with the subject of this interview.

Mitch prompted Cody to take a few photos of the building's exterior, which she did in a surprisingly random way. Once she was in her right mind again, Mitch thought, he'd send her back for more if they needed the shots. Then the two of them headed inside to the spacious, welcoming foyer. Artwork, plants, a water feature, sofas and a reception desk were blended into the building's functionality as if they were all intrinsic elements of the whole. The design felt dynamic but harmonious. Mitch permitted himself to feel somewhat impressed.

Of course there were hardly any other guests, given that Cody had insisted on arriving so early. The caterers were still organizing drinks and refreshments. A podium was still being set up, which Mitch eyed warily, having never been a fan of speeches. They were always so carefully prepared as to be meaningless.

There was no sign yet, naturally enough, of Rory Pierce.

Instead, Mitch spied various plans and drawings displayed on boards along a wide balcony on the mezzanine level. He headed up there via an attractive wide curving staircase, with Cody reluctantly following along behind, to see what information he could gather.

Half an hour later the foyer was full of guests being served by a small army of discreet waiters. There was a hum of conversation, a buzz of excitement, that even Mitch wasn't impervious to. He was taking the opportunity to interview one of the executives from the company which owned the building. Not that the exec had anything very interesting to say, but they were obviously all very pleased with themselves to have bought the talents of Rory Pierce.

Cody was next to useless, capable of little more than waiting impatiently, nervously. Mitch overheard her commenting to nobody in particular, "I couldn't even eat breakfast this morning."

Then suddenly the buzz increased. Everybody's attention diverted towards the staircase, even that of the executive.

"Wow," breathed Cody. "There he is …"

Mitch shook his head in dismay as he saw her lift her camera and watch Pierce through the lens, clicking away and taking a hundred shots. Mitch would put money on the notion that none of her photos would be any good.

But then even Mitch must turn to watch Rory Pierce walking down the staircase, making a Grand Entrance in a completely unselfconscious manner. Everybody else was tumbling over each other to get close to him. It was as if Pierce was a magnet and other people were iron filings – they aligned themselves to him.

Pierce was dressed in a dark blue suit, a colorful waistcoat, and a cream silk shirt with no tie. He obviously had an eye for style. His long dark blond hair was worn loose but perfectly groomed. The overall effect was informal but classy.

"You look stunning," said one of the reporters as Pierce came within hearing distance. "Whose suit is that?" she asked. Obviously from a fashion magazine, not the sort of title that would normally cover this kind of gig.

Pierce smiled, and replied for everybody to hear, "A new Australian label called 'Reflected Light'. You should do a feature on them, Angie. They're excellent designers."

Along with all the rest, Mitch watched Pierce closely. At first Mitch was cynical, of course, but soon he could feel the tug of seduction. He wondered if it was inevitable.

Although there were apparently some who'd rather catch Rory out than catch him. "Rory, I can't keep up with all the parties you go to," shrilled a gossip reporter. "You must be *on* something to maintain that kind of pace …"

The smile remained warm and wholehearted. "Absolutely. I'm on good food, good work, and good company. That's all it takes, Trevor."

Mitch snorted a little, hoping he wasn't wrong to sense an ironic edge to the sincerity.

The thing about Rory Pierce, Mitch found himself thinking, was that he was stunningly beautiful and obviously talented, and fully aware of his overwhelming effect on people – but he also seemed completely unpretentious. He was almost too unaffected to be true.

Pierce was on the lower reaches of the stairs now, smiling at individuals and greeting many of them by name.

One of the more serious reporters asked, "Are you disappointed with the council housing project you designed?"

Ah. Mitch's journalistic interests were piqued. That must be the low-rent housing he'd read about, that would be made available to low-income earners.

"It was a great idea, Harry," Pierce replied. "Unfortunately we didn't make it work quite as well as it could have."

The reporter persisted. "Would you get involved in another charity project like that? Or do you prefer the kind of fame and fortune this building brought you?"

Mitch winced.

But it seemed that Pierce had pretty much the perfect answer for that as well. "I'd be happy to help with more low-cost housing, if we can get the right team together. Everyone deserves to live in a properly-designed home. Actually, I think that the design becomes more important, the more modest the home. And if I didn't earn a little fame and fortune in the meantime, I wouldn't be able to contribute as much to community projects."

The shrill gossip reporter followed up on that. "Come on, Rory, he's asking a simple enough question. Which do you like best – helping the poor or working for the rich?"

The man still wasn't fazed. "Both have their rewards," Pierce replied as he made his way down to floor level, "and they're not necessarily so different. Look about you. This building can serve many good purposes. Healthy commerce might be only one of those."

Pierce was obviously heading for the podium, to take part in the afternoon's formal proceedings. On his way through the crowd, he happened to pass by Mitch and Cody, bestowing his smile on them as he did with everybody else. But a beat later, Pierce stopped and turned back to say, "Hello, Cody."

At which she almost swooned. "You remember me?"

"Of course. I remember your photography, as well – so I'm particularly glad you're here today. Do us proud, won't you?"

"Oh …"

Pierce didn't put her on the spot by expecting a sensible response. Instead, he turned to Mitch, and said, "You must be Martin Delmonaco."

Mitch shook hands with the man, and found to his chagrin that he was as speechless as Cody.

"Eva told me you'd be here today," Pierce smoothly continued. "We can start the interview once all the fuss has died down." He ducked his head a little to add with a wry smile, "Though that could take a while."

Mitch had nothing to respond with. Absolutely nothing. He watched as Pierce winked at Cody and then headed off again towards the podium. Cody began trailing after him with her camera in hand, ready for use. Mitch wouldn't even characterize her pursuit as stalking, because that implied intent, and she was simply trailing along as if attached to Pierce by a long piece of string. Well, it seemed Mitch wasn't any more immune to the glamor than anybody else … and the spell must have been particularly potent, for Mitch discovered that he couldn't even get mad at himself for that.

He didn't follow Cody into the center of attention, but instead Mitch stayed at the periphery, listening in to the gossip.

"You know who he was seen with last week?" one guest asked another in bitchy tones. "The woman who owns the 'Hellfire Club'. That'll tarnish his reputation."

"He's made of gold, darling," her companion replied. "Gold doesn't tarnish."

Another guest remarked suggestively, "He can come and redesign my home any damn time he wants."

"Oh yes, please … as long as he *personally* redecorates the bedroom."

People had gathered at the podium. Or, perhaps more to the point, they had gathered around Rory Pierce, who was at the podium. With him was the executive Mitch had been talking to earlier, along with a handful of other men and women in suits. They all looked shabby by comparison to Pierce, of course.

"Ladies and gentlemen, your attention, please …"

Mitch sighed, and pulled out his pen and notebook, so he'd be ready in the unlikely event that anything of substance was actually said.

It was a long afternoon, and Cody wasn't any kind of company at all, let alone good company. If Mitch hadn't had the interview lined up, he'd have walked out a couple of hours before. Every now and then he'd headed out to the street to light up a smoke, but he couldn't even enjoy that, anxious as he was not to miss the star of the show in all the fuss.

Eventually the other guests began leaving, still buzzing like overexcited children, and the caterers were discreetly beginning to tidy up. Everything was winding down, or maybe exhaustedly fizzling out.

Suddenly Mitch was tapped on the arm, and he spun about to find Rory Pierce beside him.

That smile was truly dizzying at close range, especially when coupled with an invitation. "Come upstairs with me."

Rory beckoned, and then led Mitch past the staircase to the elevators. Mitch found himself trailing along after the man almost without volition, just as Cody had done.

Mitch wasn't even aware of Cody, who had followed Pierce through the crowd but was now being left behind. She stalled and stood there staring after the two men, feeling quite helpless. She would have invited herself along if she'd received even the slightest encouragement – she was there on duty, after all – but Mitch didn't even think to look for her.

Then it was too late. The two men disappeared into an elevator together. And the last of the magic had gone. People began heading for the doors.

The elevator dinged to signal its arrival on the eleventh floor, and Mitch followed Rory Pierce out through the doors. Apparently nobody had yet moved into this floor, and the empty space stretched around them, large and quiet and pristine. Mitch was conscious of a hushed feeling of anticipation, and wondered whether Pierce could be aware of it, too.

They were high enough now to have a view across the city, but Mitch hardly even noticed it despite the exterior wall being almost nothing but full-length windows. If he noticed anything other than Rory Pierce himself, it was the man's work. The building's style was consistent and thorough, with the organic feel of the lobby continuing here in a subtle way. No place was left plain or ordinary and yet here, where business must become the focus, the design features weren't overwhelming or claustrophobic.

The two men wandered out onto the floor, with the sharp smell of new carpet rising from their footsteps. At some point they drifted to a halt, with about ten feet of space between them. Mitch was intrigued – far too intrigued – and Pierce ended up having to prompt him to speak.

"You wanted an interview, Mr. Delmonaco?"

Mitch forced himself to reengage like the sensible adult he actually was. "Uh, yeah. Thanks. I'm doing a feature on Sydney's architecture for the *New York Times*. I thought I'd focus on you and your work. And Eva wants a piece on this building and the opening."

"How is Eva?" Rory asked.

Mitch huffed quietly. Eva was walking wounded, but Mitch wasn't gonna get into that right now. "Uh, well, she's doing O.K."

"Good. Will you tell her I said hello? I really do appreciate this opportunity."

"Sure. Of course."

The conversation slipped back into a lull. Mitch wondered what the hell was wrong with him. He'd done this a thousand times before, but he couldn't seem to get properly started. Down in the lobby, he could attribute 'The Rory Pierce Effect' to crowd psychology, but Mitch couldn't excuse himself now that he was alone with the man.

Well. Mitch supposed that he was here to focus on Pierce anyway, so maybe he should just go with it. Finally he said, "Tell me about yourself.

Start at the beginning."

Pierce nodded, as if that wasn't an entirely unexpected request. "I was born here in Sydney. My parents were both –"

"You were *born* here?" Mitch exclaimed, interrupting. "But you've lived overseas, right? America, Europe?"

The man blinked, and said, "I've traveled."

"You must have *studied* overseas."

Pierce seemed amused by Mitch's insistence that he must have a more cosmopolitan background. "I studied in Melbourne."

"Oh." Mitch shook his head as if to clear it, and sternly reminded himself to listen. "O.K., sure. Go on, then."

Rory smiled at him. "My parents were both born here, too, but my grandparents all came from overseas: Scotland, England and Italy. I was an only child, and when I was growing up we traveled a lot – you were right about that – but mostly within Australia." He left a beat as if to give Mitch the chance to ask another question, but then continued on when he didn't. "Australia is a very old country in terms of its geology. Its shapes tend to be worn down, weathered. There's a feeling that everything has peacefully coexisted for millennia. It becomes very organic, almost quiet. The shapes, I'm talking about, not the colors. Over time it becomes balanced. Settled."

"Harmonious," Mitch suggested.

"Yes! And yet there's the dynamic sense of it all being alive and in a long-term transition. Like an old couple who've been together for decades and are still happy. It can be difficult to translate that into a modern architectural aesthetic, but I like to try."

Mitch watched and listened as if mesmerized.

Five

On the Monday Cody was oddly withdrawn, and Mitch himself was still lost in his own thoughts. They hardly spoke at all on the trip into work.

Later that morning, once he'd filed the story on Rory's building for Eva, Mitch headed down to Cody's office. He wanted to browse through her filing cabinets full of printed photos, which were arranged by general subject, looking for clues. As he'd hoped, he soon found a folder marked 'local pols', and he started flipping through it, looking for anything on the mayor.

Cody meanwhile was working away at her computer, tense in the silence as if needing to say something. Finally she asked, "So how was he … ?"

"Who?" Mitch asked absently. But then again, he reflected, who else would Cody be asking about? "Oh, Rory Pierce. Right? He was … kind of interesting."

"Interesting?" She seemed surprised. "Tell me more. Tell me everything."

But Mitch had other things on his mind. "Hey, have you heard of a guy called John Bricca? He and the mayor own a Hunter Valley vineyard."

Cody sighed. "The Hunter Valley? Beautiful place, and great wines … I think we should go investigate that in person."

"*Seriously*, Cody …"

"No, I've never heard of him." And she hadn't given up yet on her main topic of interest. "But, Marty, about Rory …"

Mitch didn't bother replying. He'd just found a photo of the mayor at a formal social event, standing in a corner out of the way, talking with a white-haired man in his fifties. The mayor was frowning uncomfortably at the camera. Mitch flipped over the photo to read Cody's notation on the back. The mystery man was identified as 'John Doe' – which surely carried the same meaning here in Australia as back in the States.

Mitch held the photo out towards Cody. "John Doe? Who's this?"

She stood up and wandered a little closer, just far enough to see. "Dunno. When I asked for his name, he actually said 'John Smith'. They both thought that was such a good joke. I, uh, didn't dignify that by writing it down. Perhaps I should have."

Mitch put the photo aside, wondering if it was actually John Bricca. Then he kept looking through the folder.

Cody opened a different drawer and pulled out a folder which she proffered in Mitch's direction. It was marked 'Rory Pierce – work'. "Why don't you concentrate on your *really* important assignment … ?"

"Yeah, right," Mitch replied on autopilot, though he felt a slight, unexpected stab of ridiculousness. "You want architecture, you go to New York or Chicago. What you have here is just quaintly derivative."

"Oh sure, I'll go," Cody retorted, "just as soon as New York has someone to compare with Rory Pierce …"

Mitch shrugged, actually letting her win that one. What was the point of arguing? He kept working through his folder of photos, while Cody sat down at her desk again and flipped idly through her photos of Rory's architecture and design work.

"Hey!" Cody suddenly exclaimed. "Here's John Doe again!"

Mitch went over to look at the photo she'd found. While the shot was of an attractive if modest block of flats, the mystery man appeared with other people mingling in the foreground, apparently unaware of the camera.

"That's the council housing project Rory designed," Cody explained.

The pang in his gut was a warning Mitch had learned to trust. "So what's this guy doing there? What's the connection?"

"I don't know."

"What was going on that day?"

She checked the back of the photo, but Cody obviously remembered. Mitch figured anything to do with Rory was probably etched on her mind. "It was the day the first people were moving in." She shot Mitch an embarrassed look. "Rory wasn't there."

Mitch extended a hand, and asked, "Mind if I hang onto these photos? The ones of John Doe or Smith or whoever he is?"

Cody wasn't precious about her work. "Take whatever you need."

Mitch returned to the filing cabinets, even more determined now to get to the bottom of this.

Late the next afternoon, Mitch was due to meet Rory at his place of business for a follow-up interview on the architecture story. By that time he was feeling rather wary.

Pierce Architecture occupied half a floor in an office building that Rory had designed. There weren't more than ten permanent staff, so there was plenty of room, and the place was full of color and natural light. A mix of clear and frosted glass separated the lift lobby from the main work area, so Mitch could see right away that the atmosphere was up-beat and stress-free. For some reason that put him even more on edge.

He let himself in through the glass doors, and was greeted by a young woman with purple hair, who seemed to cover both reception and administration. "Hello. How can I help you?"

"Martin Delmonaco. I have an appointment with Mr. Pierce."

"Of course, Mr. Delmonaco. Would you come with me?"

Rory's office was the only place that afforded any privacy, as the walls were frosted glass up to about six feet from the floor. Above that the frosting swirled into whirls and waves across the plain glass.

As Mitch was ushered in, Rory stood up from behind his desk where he'd been mulling over what appeared to be plans, and he came around to greet Mitch with his hand out to shake. "Martin. Thank you for coming."

Mitch had forgotten about the effects of that smile, especially when augmented by a firm warm handshake. "Um, yeah. Likewise," Mitch said, rather stupidly.

"Coffee?" Rory offered.

"Thanks, yeah."

The receptionist reappeared a moment later with a tray which included a pair of elegant mugs, the usual makings, and a jug of brewed coffee. The scent of it was steadying. Mitch recalled his instinctive sense of unease.

They sat opposite each other at a small round conference table, and Rory poured the coffee. When he raised a querying brow, Mitch said, "Just black. No sugar."

Rory poured milk into his own mug and then sat back, seeming perfectly at ease. "I read the piece you wrote for the *Herald* about the new building, of course. It was very thorough. Eva must be glad to have you working for her."

"She hasn't said as much."

Rory wasn't fazed by his ungraciousness. "It was well written, Martin, and I appreciate the coverage. Would you thank her for me?"

"Sure. It was her idea."

"And it's your idea to feature me in an article for the *New York Times Magazine* … ? That's very flattering, Martin."

He tersely remarked, "Yeah, if you want some real coverage, that'll do it."

There was a brief pause in which Rory considered him, finally betraying a little puzzlement over Mitch's uncooperative attitude.

Mitch tried to force himself past it. This was ridiculous. Not that he wanted to be fawning over the guy like most other people did, but neither should he be so defensive. The whole John Bricca thing was just a hunch, after all, about a trivial crime or two in a no-account city at the wrong end of the world. And even at his most cynical, Mitch didn't think Rory himself would be involved in anything nefarious, or only very peripherally at most.

Before Mitch could say anything, though, Rory offered, "I thought, if you've got the time, I could drive you around, show you a few of the projects I've worked on, tell you a bit about them."

God, Mitch would be the envy of half of Sydney. "Yeah, sure," he replied. "Whenever's convenient."

Rory smiled a bit tentatively.

Mitch dug into his satchel, hauled out a folder full of papers, and flipped through it for the photo that Cody had found. He put it on the table in front of Rory. "This is the housing project you designed, right? Low-rent council housing?"

"Right."

"Who's this guy?" Mitch asked, tapping a finger on the image of John Doe.

Rory frowned a little, and looked – and obviously recognized him. But he sat back in his chair without saying a word.

"Off the record," said Mitch.

Rory's smile broadened but turned wry. "Is anything ever really off the record with you?"

"You can trust me."

Rory gestured in the direction of the photo. "What if I can't trust him?"

"All the more reason to tell me."

"And I suppose it would only encourage you if I said he's not someone you should mess with?"

Mitch considered Rory for a long moment – and then found himself breaking into a genuine smile. "Yeah, I'm feeling encouraged, alright."

"You're as bad as Eva. Once she got her teeth into a good story, she'd never let go."

They were both grinning ruefully by now. They were actually warming to each other. Mitch's journalistic integrity seemed completely doomed when it came to this man.

"So you're saying," Mitch mused, "that I am onto a good story … ?"

"No comment," said Rory. "My God, it really is like being married again."

Mitch's nosiness got the better of him. It was such an unexpected match, Rory and Eva, and yet there had obviously been a real connection there. A connection that had persisted to some extent. "You still like her, yeah? Off the record."

Rory sobered. "I try to be her friend."

"So what went wrong?"

It seemed that this was painful for Rory, but it also seemed that he was willing to be honest. "Everyone keeps their distance, Martin, you've seen that. Even my wife kept her distance."

"I don't know – there's plenty I've seen who wanna get real close."

Rory shook his head in disagreement. "Like a wise woman once said, 'You can't dance on a pedestal'."

Mitch stared at the man for a long moment. And then he asked, "What are you doing tonight? If you can show me a decent place in this town for a drink, I'm buying."

"There are a few decent places," Rory replied.

"Then we'll try them all."

Mitch didn't have any regrets the next morning, though he was certainly feeling the effects of a night out drinking with Rory Pierce. Still, he wasn't going to let that affect his plans. He got dressed and ready a little earlier than usual, and then took his mug of coffee and cigarette out into the front courtyard. The air was already pleasantly warm, and the sky was a pure clear blue. He'd have truly appreciated it, if only he wasn't so far from home.

Mitch took a mouthful of coffee though it was still a bit too hot, and indulged in a glaring contest with the stray black cat that was still vainly loitering in the hopes of love and food. The creature obviously didn't know when to quit.

Eventually the two local beat cops walked into view, and Mitch snapped awake. "Constable! Constable Nakano, right?"

If Nakano was surprised to find that Mitch actually wanted to talk with them, she didn't show it. The two cops stopped by his front gate, and Nakano said, "Yes, that's right. Good morning, sir."

Mitch took a photo out of his suit jacket pocket, the one of John Doe talking with the mayor. "Look, I've got a photo here, I need to identify this man in it."

The two cops looked at the photo Mitch held out to them, then exchanged a significant glance. Nakano said, "His name is John Bricca."

"Good," said Mitch, tucking the photo away again. "I thought it must be."

"May I ask what your interest is?" Nakano continued, her tone calm and direct.

"Just following up a story. Don't even know if there is a story, really. He's in business with the mayor. You know about that?"

The briefest of pauses. "Are you referring to the vineyard they own, sir? As far as I'm aware, it's a legitimate business."

"O.K.," Mitch allowed, "but do you know where Bricca's money comes from?"

"No." Nakano frowned, and seemed to be considering how to say something difficult. "Mr. Delmonaco –"

But at that moment, Cody pulled up in her RAV4. "Hey, guys. Marty – God, you look awful – we're running late, come on! Eva will detonate my eardrums if I don't clock in soon. I haven't even had breakfast yet – and you know how I get if I don't eat first thing – that's how late we are."

Mitch climbed into the car still clutching his precious mug of coffee, and saluted a farewell to the cops as Cody sped off.

Adena Nakano and Jack Wethers were left staring after them.

After a moment, Wethers asked his partner, "Still think he's one of the bad guys, don't you?"

"I have my suspicions."

"But if he is, why the hell would he ask a cop about the local crims?"

"I don't know," she replied.

"If he wants to know more about them," Wethers persisted, "wouldn't he ask someone who's involved? If he wants to contact them, wouldn't he go to them directly?"

"Unless it's all double-talk, and he's trying to appear innocent."

Wethers huffed, and they resumed walking down the street. After a moment, Wethers said, "He could just be a journalist, like he said."

"Something doesn't add up. Immigration thought so, too, remember? He could just as easily be a mobster hiding out from the law."

He grinned at her fondly. "Sometimes you think too much, Adena."

"Hey, if you've got it, flaunt it!"

Meanwhile, Cody was zipping along through the usual morning traffic, taking what shortcuts she could. Mitch was hanging on tight, and trying not to spill the rest of his coffee. It was just as well he'd already drunk half of it.

Cody was silent for a while. Until she asked tersely, "Did you interview Rory yesterday afternoon?"

"Yeah," he replied. "You know, I was thinking about the next lifestyle piece –"

"You haven't finished this one yet."

"It's gonna take a while. Might as well get on with the next one at the same time."

She shot a glance at him. "More research and interviews with Rory needed, huh?"

Mitch found that he couldn't quite suppress a smile. "Yeah."

Cody was watching him carefully now, and giving the road rather less attention than she should. "How come you're looking so seedy, Marty? Were you out late last night? Drinking a bit much?"

"Yeah."

"Who with?"

Mitch sighed, and eventually reluctantly admitted, "Rory."

Cody grimaced, and for a moment she was aflame with resentment and jealousy. But then she managed to quell it all, and she glanced again at Mitch, brightening with what she obviously thought was a great idea. "Of course, you need me to do a photo-shoot with Rory for the lifestyle piece, right?"

He laughed in appreciation of her Grand Scheme. "Right. But try to get a little perspective on him, O.K.? Don't make the shots too subjective."

"Huh. You ought to listen to your own good advice, Martin, writing that article. You're already half in love with him yourself."

What … ? Mitch was stunned into silence by this assertion. Not that it was true. Obviously. But he didn't argue with her.

Not even when she concluded in tones of bitter satisfaction, "Takes one to know one."

The next time Mitch met Rory, he took him to the café in Oxford Street. That day the waiter seemed to be channeling Ellen DeGeneres, with her bleached blond short-back-and-sides, and her casual yet dapper clothes. Her easy, good-natured smile looked lovely on him.

Mitch and Rory were drinking an espresso and a latté at an outdoor table. Mitch was smoking, but making a polite effort to keep the smoke away from Rory. The café was fuller than it had been before, and all the gay men in the vicinity were staring at the beautiful Rory Pierce, unabashedly lusting after him. The ones who obviously knew who he was were avidly gossiping.

Mitch himself was also carefully watching Rory. He was still feeling unsettled by Cody's accusation that he was in love, but it was patently ridiculous. Rory was as comfortable and self-possessed as ever, and seemed to barely even notice the adulation or the examination. He just let it all flow. There was no particular personal engagement with the environment, other than as a man who was having a coffee with a friend. And that was all. It was ludicrous to think there might be more to it than that.

Eventually it was Rory who broke the silence. "How's the magazine article going, Martin?"

Mitch stirred as if surfacing from a reverie. "The architecture piece? I'm still working on it, adding depth." He found himself saying, "The more I can talk to you, the better. It's gonna be great," he concluded lamely.

"That's fine. I do appreciate it."

"Bewdy, mate," Mitch replied.

But Mitch's ironic attempt at the local lingo was met with a grimace rather than a laugh. Rory leaned in closer for the sake of discretion, and Mitch reacted by physically echoing him. "I'm concerned, though," Rory quietly said. "You asked about the man in that photo –"

"John Bricca?"

Rory looked a bit pained, as if realizing that Mitch had made progress because he now knew the man's name. "Yes. Are you including him in the article?"

"Not the one I'm doing about you. That's gonna be a 'happy happy joy joy' lifestyle magazine article. I'm looking into Bricca for an investigative piece for Eva."

Rory's worry abruptly turned to fear. "*Eva* asked you to investigate him?"

Mitch took a moment with that. Apparently it was true that Bricca shouldn't be messed with lightly. "Well, no," Mitch slowly replied. "In fact, she told me not to. But this is my job, this is what I do."

"Then you know about being careful, right?"

"Sure."

"Well, O.K. Off the record." Rory was obviously still in two minds about the matter. "Someone should look into it," he remarked, as if to himself.

"Sure," Mitch repeated. "I'm your man."

Rory's sharp gaze swung back to him, but he hadn't taken that in a personal way. "Martin, you should look into why the council housing project failed."

"It went way over budget."

"Yes, but *why* … ?"

Mitch took that on board, nodded, and sat back. The waiter approached with his insouciant Ellen-gait, and they ordered more coffee. A heavy silence stretched, which Mitch eventually made the effort to lighten.

"While I'm still pulling the architecture piece together, I'm gonna do a real fun one – *Coffee Culture*. You know, the trendy cafés everywhere, the hundred beans and blends, the thousand ways of serving it."

Rory visibly relaxed, and his smile grew. "You're crazy. A whole article on coffee?"

"Why not? Sydney ain't Seattle, but there's plenty of material. Hey, you've even got Starbucks here!"

Rory looked skeptical but willing to be persuaded. Gorgeous, too. Gorgeous, skeptical, and willing to be persuaded. It was an intoxicating mix.

Mitch and Cody spent a very long day on what she insisted on calling a 'café crawl'. Even Mitch couldn't deny that Sydney was overflowing with colorful and diverse locations in which to consume coffee. As luck would have it, they chose a particularly pleasant spring day; the sunshine was plentiful enough to require them to wear sunglasses and look cool throughout. It didn't take long at all before even Mitch was jazzed on too much espresso. They sampled different styles of coffee everywhere they went, along with all kinds of coffee-flavored cakes and chocolates. The abundance of caffeine and sugar ensured a manic kind of fun. The owners and baristas, waiters and customers were all happy to chat and to oblige with recipes, information and anecdotes. By midday Mitch had more than enough notes, and Cody more than enough photos – including several self-portraits on her phone's camera, with both of them grinning up at it like lunatics. Perhaps they should have quit while they were ahead.

It all ended on a sour note, when Mitch cast a cynical eye over an urban café's clientele. There were yuppies dressed identically, all with cell phones; there were scruffy deadbeats from the local college; there were gossiping mothers with their impatient children in strollers. Mitch found himself reacting as if he had a bad taste in his mouth. "And we're calling this *culture*? Jeez …"

Six

In the cool of early morning the next day, Mitch could be found sitting at an outdoor café table at the local shops near where he lived. He was staring balefully at yet another espresso, and smoking a cigarette with his hand slightly shaking. His laptop, cell phone and morning newspapers were all sitting there awaiting his attention, and he was ignoring them. Was it possible to be hung-over from an overindulgence in coffee, Mitch pondered, or could his current state be more accurately attributed to sleep deprivation?

"Good morning, Mr. Delmonaco."

The greeting was patiently repeated, and Mitch finally looked up. A young woman stood there considering him with a wary kind of sympathy. It took Mitch a moment to place her because she was in civilian clothes. "Ah, Constable Nakano … Good morning. I didn't recognize you without your sidekick and nightstick."

She smiled benignly, and then indicated the café with a nod. "They serve good coffee here. I don't think I'd survive the late shift without it."

"Yeah, well, with the amount I've drunk lately, I don't think I'm gonna sleep for a week."

But that was enough social chitchat, apparently. "How's the story progressing?"

"Good, actually. Certainly well-fueled." He sketched a wide if somewhat sloppy grin for her. "Oh, I'm writing one about coffee, but you mean the Bricca thing, right?"

"Right."

"And this is where you tell me to proceed with caution?"

"Right again."

His grin now was smaller but more genuine. "You know, you're all just piquing my interest with these warnings."

She frowned. "Who else have you been talking to?"

Mitch intoned with some irony, "I cannot reveal my sources."

Which prompted Nakano to sit down at his table uninvited. "Well, what have you got so far?"

Mitch forced himself to sit up straighter. He wasn't going to let an opportunity go by, even if he did feel like he'd OD'd at lethal levels. "Not much. Lots of suspicions. Lots of speculation about where all his money's coming from. A few leads."

"You take care," she advised, not looking overly relieved despite this admission that he was getting nowhere. "He'd be ugly enough on his own, but he's not the only one involved."

Mitch wasn't too poorly to put two and two together. "Ah, so you've got organized crime down here in Australia. How cute."

"No cuter than your lot in the States. You get on the wrong side of ours, you're just as dead." Nakano stared hard at him for a moment. "Or are you looking for a way in on the *right* side of them?"

"What … ?"

"I don't think you're quite who you say you are, Mr. Delmonaco."

What the … ?! Mitch sat up straighter still. "Who the hell do you think I am?"

"I don't know."

"I'm a journalist. I'm an American. That's the truth."

Nakano stood up, ready to go. "Good, then. I hope so." She leaned forward to tap at the table to emphasize her point. "Be careful, Mr. Delmonaco. And tell me what you find."

Mitch stared after her as she strode away, feeling utterly disconcerted. Could she really think he was looking for a way in … ? Surely not.

Maybe he'd misinterpreted. Over-interpreted. No doubt he'd just had too much caffeine in the past twenty-four hours. Mitch pushed the untouched espresso away, and dropped a couple of two-dollar coins in the saucer.

As he was standing he saw Cody's RAV4 coming down the street, so he quickly gathered up his laptop, phone and papers, and waved for her to stop.

Still dressed in her casual clothes, Adena Nakano strode into the police station, swiped through security, and headed for her desk.

"Adena, what's up?" one of her colleagues asked. "I thought you were on the late shift this week."

"There's something I'm gonna get to the bottom of," she replied. "It's been nagging at me for weeks." She started flipping through a folder of contact phone numbers, while waiting for her computer to boot up. "Anyone know what time it is in America right now? The east coast."

One of the others said, "Aren't they twelve or fourteen hours behind us? Something like that."

Adena soon found what she wanted. "Never mind, it's listed as a twenty-four hour number." She picked up the land-line handset, and dialed.

Two rings later, the call was answered. "Justice Department." The voice was male, and sounded friendly enough, but Adena knew he wouldn't give away a millimeter more than he had to.

"I need someone in the Witness Protection Program, please."

"You can talk to me."

"This is Constable Adena Nakano, New South Wales Police Force, warrant number 60023. I'm calling from Australia."

"Yes."

The terse responses weren't unexpected, but were still somewhat disconcerting. "Uh, I'm calling about a U.S. citizen currently living here, name of Martin Delmonaco. I need to know if he's connected with your program."

"Why?"

"Why?" she repeated, the frustration of the situation sharpening her tone. "Because there's more to him than meets the eye. Because I wouldn't be surprised if that's not his real name. Because if I know he's one of yours then I can stop worrying."

There was the briefest pause, as if the W.P.P. officer was merely making sure she'd finished talking, then he said, "I can neither confirm nor deny that he's one of ours."

"Well, put me onto someone who can."

"I'm sure you understand that nobody here can or will help you, Constable."

Adena took a moment to swallow a retort. "Alright," she eventually said. "Point taken. But you listen to this – if he's one of yours, you watch out for him. He's sticking his nose where it isn't wanted."

There was no immediate response, and Adena didn't wait for one, either. "Goodbye," she said, and hung up.

She sat back in her chair, and let the surge of irritability fade. She thought for a moment. And then she stood and headed for the locker room.

Adena arrived in the lobby of the *Sydney Morning Herald* dressed in her full uniform. The security guard at reception didn't even blink, but handled her request calmly and efficiently. Within moments Adena was being escorted to the office of editor Eva Lewis.

Eva stood up from her desk when Adena was shown in, but didn't offer to shake hands. "Hello," she said coolly. "I'm Eva Lewis. How can I help you?"

Adena identified herself, and showed her badge and warrant card. She was mildly shocked to find that Eva was smoking. "This is a public building," Adena remarked. "By law, it's a non-smoking building."

"Is *that* what this is about?" Eva's look was flatly ironic, as if she already knew the answer.

"No. I'm just curious. How do you even get away with that anymore?"

Eva merely shrugged, and indicated that Adena should take a visitor's chair. Adena sat, and took out her pen and notebook just in case. Eva sat as well, with the desk between them, and when she was done smoking the current cigarette, she lit up another one.

It didn't take long for Adena to explain her business. She noted with interest that Eva didn't betray a hint of surprise to hear Adena's suspicions – which in itself told her plenty.

Eva's verbal responses were rather less informative. "Mr. Delmonaco is doing good work for me," she insisted. "I haven't had cause to question him."

"So you can confirm he's a journalist."

"Yes, for the fourteenth time," Eva irritably replied.

"But you won't tell me anything else."

Eva took a long drag on her cigarette. "He came highly recommended."

"By whom?"

No reply was offered. Adena was feeling more and more frustrated. Eva was looking colder and colder, and as if to underscore her lack of welcome she was pretty much chain-smoking.

Adena finally continued, "I'm going to find out sooner or later, Ms. Lewis. You might think you're helping him, but you're not."

Eva acknowledged this with a lift of her chin, and became ever so slightly less annoyed. "I know what it's like to get the scent of a story, Constable. But I also know when to listen to people. Mr. Delmonaco has done nothing wrong."

"Then where's the harm in me knowing more?"

"You're not that naïve," Eva said, "or you wouldn't be wearing that uniform. If you dig deeper you could put him in danger, and you'd only have yourself to blame. I don't think you want that."

Adena left a long pause, which Eva was too self-contained to fill. Eventually Adena said, "I'm concerned about Mr. Delmonaco's true identity, but I'm also concerned that he's the one who's digging too deep."

Eva didn't say anything, but she was obviously listening.

"He's got the scent of a story about John Bricca. I don't know what Mr. Delmonaco is chasing exactly, but you can imagine the sort of thing it might be as well as I can." Adena concluded, "You'd do better protecting him from Bricca than from me."

Eventually Eva nodded her agreement. At least one point had been taken.

Adena stood and handed over a business card. "Thank you for your time, Ms. Lewis. If there's anything you think I need to know, or anything I can help with, please call me."

Eva took the card, and Adena didn't bother waiting for any further acknowledgement.

Of course, as soon as Adena reached the floor of the newsroom, she heard the cry, "Yo! Constable!" in a distinctly American accent. She looked across to see Martin Delmonaco standing at a distant desk, and raising a hand to catch her attention. Almost everyone else in the room had turned mildly curious stares on them both, and now waited on her reaction. Adena indulged in a reluctant glare, but figured she had no choice but to go over.

"Look, Constable," Delmonaco was saying as soon as she was within earshot of a voice at a regular volume, "I'm a real journalist. Here's my desk, here's my computer, and my laptop, here's a pen and my notebook – which I swear you've seen me use, by the way. You can check my notes about that policy launch you were at, right? They even gave me a cell phone, though I don't know who the hell's gonna be calling me." He faltered, as if realizing that wasn't such a wise admission. "I mean, people tend to use the land-line, yeah?"

She stood there with her hands shoved in her jacket pockets. Eventually she said, "The job could be a cover."

Martin grabbed a nearby copy of the *Herald*, leafed through it, and then showed her an article with a 'Martin Delmonaco' byline. Adena hauled over a spare chair, and sat down to read it. Meanwhile, Martin opened up other newspapers, and passed them over – but Adena sighed and didn't pick them up. "O.K., I know you can write. It could still be a cover."

"It's not a cover, it's my life. I've been a journalist since I was five years old, and wrote an obituary for the goldfish our cat ate."

Despite herself, Adena smiled. "I'm not necessarily saying you're a bad person, Mr. Delmonaco."

"But if you're willing to accept that I'm a good person, then don't you think I'd have my own very good reasons for being here and doing this?"

She considered him carefully, torn between conflicting instincts. "You're asking me to leave well enough alone."

"Yeah, I am."

"Well," she said, "maybe I will if you will."

Delmonaco finally sat down again. "You mean the Bricca thing? But he's not one of the good guys, Constable. Why wouldn't you want me to follow up on that?"

"Even if I accept you're a journalist, and this is a legitimate job, I know it's not the whole story."

Delmonaco let out a sigh. "Well, I guess if you can't trust me or take Eva's word for it, then we each have to do what we've got to do and let the chips fall where they may."

The two of them looked at each other, knowing they'd reached an impasse.

Adena stood to go. "Thank you for your time, Mr. Delmonaco." She handed him a business card, and left him staring down at it tiredly.

Mitch arrived home at last after an enervating day, with a bag of groceries hanging heavily from one hand, his satchel slung over the opposite shoulder, and a cigarette held firm between his lips. He glared sourly at the stray cat still loitering in his courtyard. He'd finally got the knack of unlocking the front door, so he managed that one-handed and then closed it firmly behind him.

A moment later he re-emerged, however, with a small can of cat food.

He opened it using the pull tab, and put it down on the front steps, before backing away and brusquely beckoning to the cat. "Come on, then. Live it up while you can."

The cat's hunger soon overrode its wariness, and it stepped over and started eating. Between mouthfuls, however, the cat still cast Mitch suspicious looks, and it seemed its hackles were ready to rise as soon as needed.

"I hope my invited guests won't be so ungrateful," Mitch remarked.

A happy laugh sounded, along with the remark, "I see the stray American has been adopted."

Mitch looked up to see Rory Pierce standing on the sidewalk watching this little tableau with some amusement. Mitch found himself smiling quite uncomplicatedly. "Hey! Are you early or am I late, or both? I only just got home. Come in and have a drink."

"Love to," said Rory. And he followed Mitch inside.

Mitch poured them each a shot of whiskey, while trying in vain to organize his groceries and work stuff, conversing all the while. He had to admit that he felt a little … flustered. That was the description his journalistic integrity demanded. Mitch found that being around Rory Pierce these days … flustered him. It was a somewhat alarming development.

"You'll have to excuse my horribly humble abode," Mitch was babbling. "Nothing an award-winning architect could possibly be impressed by, of course – and even I try not to spend too much time here."

But Rory was looking about quite happily. "Nah, actually I like these old places."

"You do?"

"I do. It's fun redesigning them. Bringing them back to life. Some we do traditionally, of course, but one project I worked on, we knocked the whole interior out and started again from scratch."

Mitch huffed ironically. "Yeah, well, I guess I can see the attraction of that. Cleaning the slate, starting over."

Rory cast him a curious glance, as if wondering whether the sentiment applied to more than rebuilding work.

Mitch changed the subject. "Look, are we gonna be late for dinner?"

"It doesn't matter," Rory said quite easily.

Oh yeah, Mitch thought, people probably let this guy get away with anything. "One of the benefits of being a celebrity, huh?"

But Rory shrugged this off, as if the comment was meaningless.

Mitch took a long swallow of whiskey, and looked about him at the uninspiring dining room, with the poky little kitchen running off it. He changed the subject back again. "Tell me what you were saying before about architecture being sexy … ?"

Rory responded to that with a grin. "It's about how your body relates to the world," he explained in tones that edged into the suggestive. "It's about how we interact with each other. It's like how clothes are sexy, but on a larger scale."

Mitch's full attention was on Rory, who was not unaware of it.

"If you really look at a building," Rory continued, coincidentally wandering closer to Mitch, "it's all about rhythm and space … rhythm and space … rhythm and space."

Mesmerizing. Rory Pierce might actually be flirting with him. What were the odds on that?

Mitch shook himself back into the real world, and grasped at the next available subject. "Oh God, that reminds me," he blurted. "Cody said we need a photo-shoot to go with the article. For the *Times* piece, you know?"

Rory's grin twisted a little. "Of me or the buildings?"

"What do you think?" Mitch responded with a humorless laugh. "It's not architecture she finds sexy. But is that gonna be O.K. with you?"

"Yes, of course it's O.K.," Rory said sincerely. His face had cleared of any wryness or irony. "Cody's a really good photographer, you know. She has an eye for the telling detail. Ask her to call the office and set up a time."

"She'll think it's Christmas." Oh my God, he thought. Again with the blurts! "And she'd kill me if she knew I said that. Uh, let's just get out of here before I shove my foot in any deeper."

Rory, of course, was smiling, unafraid and unoffended. He put down his whiskey glass next to Mitch's, and then followed as Mitch headed out the front door. Moments later, the two men climbed into Rory's well-loved vintage MG, and sped away.

Seven

All the warnings about John Bricca had had two effects on Mitch. One was to intrigue him, but the other was a determination not to involve Cody any further. When Mitch went to visit the council housing project that Rory had been part of, therefore, he took a cab. Not without some regret, but really it was beneath his dignity to become so reliant on having his own personal chauffeur.

Mitch was soon missing Cody for other reasons as well, though. He wanted to question a number of residents, to see if he could gain another fact or two – or even just an inference – about John Bricca's involvement in the project. And so he began knocking on doors and introducing himself.

Nobody was at all cooperative. Nobody did anything but glare at him, tell him where to go, and slam the door in his face. Perhaps it was the Yank thing. Perhaps it was the lack of a friendly face. No doubt Cody would have known what to say or do, to allay suspicions.

To his surprise, Mitch also missed Cody's ubiquitous camera. The building seemed pleasant, and well-designed both practically and decoratively. It was clear, however, that there were already some repairs needed. Mitch couldn't help but conclude it had been built on the cheap. He managed to figure out how to use the camera on his cell phone in order to capture some of the details, but God only knew if the photos would be of any use.

At last, just as Mitch was about to give up on finding someone to interview, one of the residents replied, "Yes. I'll talk with you."

"Oh. That'd be great, thanks."

"Come in, please," the young man said, stepping back and holding the door open wide.

Mitch walked into the apartment. Not that he didn't have misgivings. The young man conveyed the innocent sort of trust that meant Mitch would need to tread very carefully. Still, presumably he had a carer or companion of some sort in there, who'd ensure nobody was taken advantage of.

Mitch looked around what must be the main room. The place was clean, and would have been almost empty but for the many model train tracks running across and around the floor, and apparently through the whole apartment. Mitch was about to take a step further in when he was startled by a train running past his feet. Instead he carefully turned on the spot to find his host.

The young man asked, "May I make you a coffee, Mister, uh … I've forgotten your name."

"I'd love a coffee, thanks, and you can call me Martin."

He gaped in surprise. "But that's my name!"

Mitch grinned at him. "Well, it's mine, too."

Martin seemed delighted that they had this in common. "May I make you a coffee, Martin?"

"Yeah, thanks, that'd be great." As Martin headed for what must be the kitchen, Mitch called after him, "Are you on your own here, or do you have family with you?"

"No. I live here on my own," was the reply. "I'm old enough now, you know."

"I don't doubt it," said Mitch. The guy must be in his twenties at least, and was obviously capable of taking care of himself, at least on the domestic side of life. Mitch felt some qualms about interviewing him on what could be a contentious subject, but he'd take it slow and careful. Ordinarily he'd have probably decided to leave well enough alone, but he was getting desperate for something – anything – about John Bricca.

While Martin was boiling the kettle and making coffee – only instant, Mitch realized, but he wasn't going to complain – Mitch settled in an easy chair and got out his notebook. A few minutes later Martin returned with two mugs of coffee, which he placed on an otherwise empty small table; then Martin folded down to sit cross-legged on the floor. Mitch belatedly realized he himself was sitting in the only chair.

"You alright down there?" he asked.

"Yes. I always sit here," Martin replied with a smile. He indicated the train track running past his shins. "Because of the trains."

"I see." Mitch smiled at the guy, and then finally launched into the interview. "O.K. … Martin, do you know somebody named John Bricca?"

"Yes. Mr. Bricca is a nice man, he helped me when I wanted to live here. It's my home now."

"That's good. So how exactly is he involved in the building?"

Martin looked at Mitch blankly.

Mitch tried rephrasing. "Was he helping the council? Was he helping the builders? Is he on the body corporate?"

"Yes. Mr. Bricca helped everyone. He's a nice man. Of course he said I shouldn't tell anyone I know him, or answer any questions."

"Or he'd do what … ?"

Martin didn't seem to think this follow-up at all odd. "He just said I shouldn't answer any questions."

"But you said you'd answer my questions."

"Yes. You're a nice man, too." Martin sat there looking up at Mitch, thoroughly and honestly ingenuous.

Mitch considered the guy for a long moment. A model train whistled and ran towards Mitch, under his chair, and out again.

Finally Mitch decided he couldn't risk getting this young man into trouble. Mitch smiled, and slid his notebook away. "Thank you, Martin. That's all I need to know."

"You're welcome. You can ask me more questions if you would like. I don't mind."

"Well, uh, why don't you tell me about all your trains here? Then when Mr. Bricca asks if anybody's been asking any questions, you can tell him that you just told me about your trains, and nothing more. Alright?"

"Yes," said Martin – though Mitch didn't hold much hope of Martin not just telling Bricca everything. Still, perhaps there was the chance that Bricca would be swamped in chat about model trains, and not think it worth pursuing any further.

"This is a copy of the Oriental Express, it goes real fast, except when I don't keep the track clean, it takes a lot of time to keep the tracks clean –"

Mitch sipped at the coffee, lit up a cigarette, and gave Martin at least half of his attention.

That didn't accomplish much, so Mitch's next stop was the council offices – where he didn't even get past the receptionist in the foyer.

"All I'm asking for," Mitch ended up clarifying with what little patience he could muster, "is to look at the accounts for that housing project. It's not a difficult request."

She was singularly unimpressed. "And I told you already, they're not available at the moment." She let a beat go by before asking in tones that completely undermined the polite phrasing, "May I ask what your interest is?"

"What my interest is? Jeez, haven't you ever heard of public scrutiny down here?"

"The accounts are thoroughly audited. That particular building company is scrupulous, and always have their accounts audited before handing them over."

If she'd meant to deflate any suspicions, she was going the wrong way about it. Mitch remarked, "Sounds like they're covering something up ..."

"Sounds like an overactive imagination," she snapped in return.

Mitch let out something that was more a groan than a sigh. "Look, I get that you don't like me. It's been a frustrating day, and I guess I'm not very likable at the best of times. But can we put that aside for now? This is about government business and taxpayer's money. I'll submit a Freedom of Information request, if I have to, and you won't be able to obstruct *that*."

She'd been looking at Mitch as if she still thought him a smart-ass, despite the attempted mollification.

It belatedly occurred to Mitch that this outpost of civilization might be somewhat lagging in legislation. "You do *have* F.O.I. down here, right?"

"Yes, we do," she brusquely replied. "Good luck, Mr. Delmonaco, and goodbye."

He glared at her one last time, and headed for the door.

Well, Mitch reflected, he still had one source he hadn't managed to antagonize yet. On the sidewalk outside the council offices, he pulled out his cell phone and tapped in a number he already knew by heart. Then he held the phone against one ear with his shoulder, so he could also juggle his notebook and pen. The voice which answered sounded to Mitch like sanity personified.

"Hey, Rory, it's Martin. Got a minute?"

"Of course. What's up?"

"Knight Construction, the building company who put up your housing project – what other work have they done?"

Rory didn't even let a beat go by. "Can you hold for a few minutes? Or shall I call you back? I'll get some addresses for you."

"Thanks. That's cool, I'll hold. Oh, and if you know any of the owners I could contact, I'd appreciate names."

"No worries. Hang on, Martin."

Mitch hung on.

Another cab dropped Mitch off in front of another nondescript office building. He looked up at it, as unimpressed by this one as the others he'd visited that day, and then he headed inside. Soon he was in a rather shabby office, interviewing a guy named Jones. And the great thing was that Jones was disgruntled enough to want to talk.

"You see that?" Jones asked, pointing up to where a ceiling tile was missing. "That tile almost fell on a client's head the other day. This whole place is second rate. Looked good enough when we moved in, but then all the cracks started showing."

Mitch nodded, and asked, "How do you explain that?"

"It's the building company. 'We stand by our work,' they say. So we sign a maintenance contract with them – and a damned costly one at that. They get a regular income out of it. Hell, it might be the only thing keeping them afloat."

"Last guy I spoke to said much the same. Have you heard of a John Bricca?"

Jones thought for a moment, and shook his head. "No. What, he's with Knight Construction?"

"I don't know yet," Mitch replied.

When Mitch emerged from the office building, he got the distinct impression he was being watched. It wasn't one of those hackles-up instincts so much as the fact there was a car parked across the street and the driver was staring at him. The guy even seemed to be reporting something into a cell phone. His expression was quite blank, however, and he didn't react to Mitch staring back at him. No doubt it was just a coincidence.

After a long moment the guy put down the phone, pulled out into the passing traffic, and drove off. Mitch watched him go, but soon turned away.

He figured that sometimes it did all come down to his imagination working overtime.

Meanwhile, the local council election campaigns wound along their weary way. One afternoon Mitch and Cody were at a suburban shopping mall, loitering on the fringes of a small crowd who'd gathered to listen to one of the 'least likely to' candidates. Again, the main attraction seemed to be the food, with cakes and other baked goods for sale, and freshly made silver dollar pancakes – that Cody called 'pikelets' – available for free. Neither Mitch nor Cody were interested in patronizing the various stalls, so they were thoroughly bored.

After a lengthy silence, Cody asked, "So … how come you haven't been using your personal chauffeur service lately?"

Mitch looked at her. "You don't wanna be driving me around all the time."

"I don't mind."

"And people tell me *I* don't have a life …" Mitch wanted to change the subject, because he knew Cody would insist on being involved if he told her about his further investigations into John Bricca. Luckily, he knew just how to divert her. "Did you set up that photo-shoot with Rory yet?"

Cody couldn't help but break into a happy grin. "Yeah. He's coming over next Wednesday."

"Coming over?" Mitch wondered if the term carried the same implication in Australia as in the States. "You don't mean to your place, do you?"

"Yeah, I do." Cody glanced at him sidelong, but continued as if this were absolutely reasonable. "Remember I told you I converted the main room in my apartment to a studio? I'm on the top floor, lots of natural light."

God, where did he even begin this argument? "You should photograph him in his buildings. Amidst the design features. The man and his work."

"But location shoots are such a pain," she came back smoothly. "You gotta cart around all this lighting and equipment, I'd need to take a couple of extra guys with me –"

"And this way you're alone with him, right?"

"Right," Cody agreed, looking unbearably smug.

Mitch felt almost too annoyed to respond. The wannabe politician was droning on in the background. Mitch finally growled through gritted teeth, "And you have the balls to accuse *me* of being too subjective about him."

They shared an irritable glare, and then returned their attention to the politician.

Pursuing his own investigations again into John Bricca and Knight Construction, Mitch soon found himself interviewing a building supplier named Valeri. He seemed a decent guy, and was definitely prepared to talk. Perhaps he'd even been waiting for a chance to do so.

"Yeah, there's something rotten in the state of Knight Construction. I gave them supplies at cost for that housing project, and I donated the delivery. It was a charitable thing, see? Lumber, plasterboard, nails, glue, you name it. A lot of hardware. And I mean a *bloody* lot of it."

"That's good of you," said Mitch, "but I'm missing the significance."

"Well, it niggled at me for a while, but then I started getting an idea or two about that outfit and it suddenly clicked."

"What did?"

Valeri stood a little taller as if to underscore his point. "They could have used the excess supplies in their commercial sites. Or sold them elsewhere at retail prices. Might not seem like much to you, but if I wasn't the only supplier who got taken for a ride it could really add up."

"Ah," Mitch said with a nod. "Yeah, that'd be a pretty good scam. Did you tell anybody?"

"I talked to a cop, but he couldn't do anything. Well, couldn't or wouldn't. Not that I blame him. It's all just suspicions on my part. I kept an eye out, but I never saw anything to prove it either way."

That seemed to be that, so Mitch asked, "Did you ever hear of a John Bricca?"

Valeri nodded right away. "Yeah, he was involved, I don't really know how. A friend of someone. Sometimes he acted like a spokesman or a fixer or something."

"A fixer for what? Or for who?"

"I really don't know. I didn't pay him much attention. The few things I was involved in, he kind of kept his head down. Stayed in the background." Then something occurred to Valeri. "But one time he was there … There were blokes clocking in for work, and I swear they'd never picked up a brick in their lives. Clean hands, smart clothes, and the kind of tans you pay for. They hung around for a while, and when they left they didn't clock out. Maybe they came back to do that later." Valeri left a significant pause before adding, "I've heard Knight Construction pays premium rates, too."

Mitch tried to suppress his excitement, but he felt like he was finally digging into the good stuff that he'd known all along was there. "That's great."

"Yeah." Valeri considered him for a long moment. "You're gonna do something about this, right?"

"I'm gonna damn well try."

Once Mitch was back at the *Herald* offices, he used the land-line to call Tom Lewis's cell phone. It was early evening in Sydney, so it was almost the middle of the night for Tom – but not so late that Mitch thought he wouldn't still be awake.

Tom, however, was majorly unimpressed. "Take pity on an old man, Mitch. I was fast asleep."

"Sorry, but –"

"This really can't wait?"

"Well." Mitch took a breath, but either the story was urgent or Mitch himself was selfish. Maybe both. "I don't wanna wait," he said with relative honesty.

"And I don't wanna wake the missus. Hang on."

Mitch waited for a few moments while Tom apparently got out of bed and headed for a different room. Mitch took the opportunity to light a cigarette.

Finally Tom said, "Alright. This better be good."

"Yeah, it is. I've really stumbled onto something, Tom. There's a building company, into all kinds of shady deals – cheap construction, expensive maintenance contracts, making money off donated supplies –"

Tom interrupted him. "They call that Standard Operating Procedure."

Mitch huffed. "You're not that cynical, Tom, you're just tired."

"So get to the point, damn it!"

"It's not just a shonky building company – I think they're a front for the local mob, money-laundering and all."

"*Shonky?*" Tom repeated. "They've got you talking Strine already?"

"Can you believe they actually have organized crime down here? It's like a cute little baby mob."

Tom let out a sigh. "For God's sake, Mitch, when are you gonna start taking anything outside of Manhattan *seriously?* I told you no more exposés."

"But, Tom –"

"Go interview Elle Macpherson or something. New Yorkers will love reading about her. Let Eva handle this mob story."

"I'm still covering the local council elections, would you believe? Thank God they're voting next Saturday. Even covering public health insurance would be better than this. It's federal politics at least. Or tele-communications – that's always an issue."

"Forget it," Tom gruffly replied. "You need to keep your head down."

Mitch left a pause. There was no denying he felt tired, and maybe one or two of his usual barriers were down. He took a long drag on the last of his cigarette and stubbed it out. Eventually he asked, "Did you ever meet Rory Pierce … ?"

"No," Tom replied in slightly softer tones. "No, I didn't. I just saw Eva afterwards, she worked for us for a while in the L.A. bureau. She was a bloody wreck, Mitch."

"I don't think it's his fault," Mitch mused. "Not that it was hers, either. If you met him –"

"If I met him, I'd knock his fuckin' head off his shoulders. Then I might let him apologize."

Obviously it was time for a tactical retreat. "Yeah, well, Tom, I'll let you get back to sleep."

"Mitch, please don't tell me –"

"Goodnight, Tom."

"– I gotta warn *you* off him?!"

Mitch gingerly hung up the phone.

Cody had carefully prepared her main living room for the photo-shoot with Rory. All of her equipment was set up, the lighting was in place, and the first of her chosen backdrops was hanging ready. She'd taken down and safely stored most of the images of Rory she'd had pinned to one wall, but she'd left a few as points of reference. Often it was easier to discuss an idea or an emotion with a visual clue as to what she did or didn't intend. In any case, he knew well enough she had a crush on him. Cody wasn't going to pretend to be anything she was not.

He arrived perfectly on time, on his own, and – though she hadn't prompted him – with a few changes of clothes in a garment bag. "Hello, Cody," Rory said with a smile.

"Hello." She hung the bag from one of the coat hooks near the door, unzipped it and quickly looked through at the various colors and textures. When she turned back to look at him, she concluded he must have also had his hair cut within the last day or two. "This is very professional of you."

"I blame the Scouts," he quipped. "You know, 'Be Prepared'? They were a major influence in my formative years."

Cody grinned at him, and tried to think of something witty to say about earning merit badges – but nothing would come, so instead she offered him coffee which he gladly accepted.

From there they seemed to naturally progress into taking a few test shots in order to fine-tune the lighting, and then starting to take some proper shots in what Rory was already wearing. He seemed friendly and relaxed, willing to put in the time and effort and yet also willing to have fun. Before Cody knew it, they were both having fun.

Most of the shots were simply of Rory in various moods, with changes in his clothes and the backdrop. In some, though, they tried for artier effects using props such as blueprints, printed photos of the buildings he'd designed, a pair of compasses and so on.

To Cody's amazement they were happy in each other's company, and she felt sure that the photos would be all the better for that. They were even flirting, a little, though of course that would be due more to the inherent eroticism of the process rather than Rory suddenly feeling a partiality … Every time it occurred to Cody that Rory was actually enjoying himself, she told herself not to think about it. Thinking about it would lead to doubt, and doubts would create fear, and fear would undermine the shaky foundations of this oh-so-temporary construction. Cody decided to give herself the gift of not stuffing it up.

They ended up taking more photos than necessary, and some were far more personal than the magazine would want to use. Some were even intimate, in an emotional way.

Cody had never had a better time in her life.

They weren't done until well into the evening. Finally it occurred to them both, as Cody frowned and went to reset the lights, that it was dark outside already. "Time flies …" murmured Rory.

"It does," she quietly agreed. This was all going to be over in a minute or two. "I think – I think that some of these photos will be –"

"Exceptional," he supplied, and then smiled when she looked at him. "I'm starving!" Rory declared. "Shall we order in, do you think, or shall we go out?" When she didn't immediately reply, he added, "Of course, you have plans –"

"No. No plans. I was thinking – I could cook for you. If you don't mind something simple, like a stir-fry?"

"I'd love it. Thank you."

And so the perfections of the afternoon segued into Rory fuckin' Pierce sitting in her tiny kitchen, contentedly drinking a glass of crisp white wine and watching while Cody cooked for him. She'd hardly dared imagine …

They chatted and talked through dinner and afterwards. But then later, when they were sitting in near-darkness in the main room, looking out across the city lights, they fell silent.

Eventually Cody put down her glass of wine, and turned to Rory, and pressed a kiss to his mouth. He wasn't surprised, but responded, a little. In turn she deepened the kiss into something that was tentatively passionate. He was carefully gentle in meeting her advances and never making any of his own. Finally she drew away, and stared at him with fear and hope.

He whispered, "Is this really a good idea?"

"Best one I've ever had," she replied.

He gazed at her for long moments, and she conveyed nothing but an easy confidence. At last Rory put any doubts aside, and they kissed again. It was the most perfect thing in the world.

Later, in the dark of night, she felt differently. In some ways, she thought, she didn't feel anything at all. She was oddly numb.

She'd dozed for a while, and then woken up next to Rory, who was deeply asleep. Strange, the contrast between his utter comfort and her restlessness, her unhappiness. She didn't know how to deal with that.

She lay there, wide awake, for a while. When that became unbearable she carefully eased out of the bed, picked up her camera, and curled up in the armchair in the corner of the room. She watched him through the lens, which felt somewhat less strange, composing and focusing various images. There was just enough light coming in through the window as she never closed the blinds. She actually took a picture or two. She could delete them later, if she needed to. Then she just watched him some more.

Eventually, she fell asleep in the armchair.

The early morning found Cody in her kitchen brewing coffee. She was almost shaking with nerves and felt as fragile as an eggshell.

Perhaps scenting the coffee Rory stumbled in, still half asleep. Still wholly adorable. She looked at him, wide-eyed, and he came over to give her a hug, press a kiss to her hair – but she shrugged him off, and instead passed him a mug of coffee.

It was painful to see Rory politely withdraw, both physically and emotionally. Cody watched, wondering how on earth she could want such a thing. And yet she did. If he was hurt it would only be a little bit, and he certainly didn't betray it to her. But why, she asked herself, would she want to hurt Rory Pierce?

"Uh," she eventually said, "I hope coffee will do, 'cos I never eat breakfast."

Which was an absolute lie, but he wasn't to know that.

"This is great coffee," he replied with exactly the right sort of warm urbanity. "That's absolutely fine. Thanks, Cody."

They each silently sipped at the coffee, waiting through these difficult moments.

Finally Rory was ready to go, with the gear he'd brought the day before. He was smiling regretfully, but Cody couldn't tell if that was genuine or only polite. At the front door it seemed as if he wanted to kiss Cody goodbye, but she managed to avoid any contact with him. Then he was gone, and the door was firmly closed.

For a moment, Cody felt utterly stranded. A brief storm of tears beset her.

But then she calmed again. After a moment she headed for the drawer in which she'd put away the other photos of Rory, and she began putting them back up on the wall one by one. Her face felt still now, as if it were a mask. She knew that that was a good thing.

Eight

Mitch was outside in his little courtyard, feeding the stray cat and refilling its water bowl. There was the usual cool, quiet hush to the early morning, which he knew would soon be lost in the day's warmth and the city's busyness. He tried to enjoy the sense of peace while he could.

Cody drove up right on time, and parked in the street. She got out of the car, gathered up her bag of photography equipment, slung her camera round her neck, and walked over to wait on the sidewalk, leaning one hip against Mitch's courtyard wall.

"Hey, Cody," Mitch said. "This is gonna be a good story. Figure I'll call it *A Day in the Life of a Beat Cop*. Obvious but true. There's no point in trying to be clever for these pieces. They work better when they're straightforward." Finally, once the cat was sorted, he stood up and considered Cody properly. "Hey, you don't look so great."

"Gee, thanks," she responded sarcastically.

Mitch examined her a little more closely. Cody's moods and sleep patterns were always all over the place, but that morning her face was unusually drawn and pale. "I didn't mean it like that, and you know it. Are you O.K.?"

"Yeah, I'm fine."

"I've hardly even seen you since – Hey, how did the much anticipated photo-shoot go?"

"It went fine," she replied with mild irritation. "Lots of photos. I'll sort out the best for you when we get to the office."

"O.K.," he said, though he was wondering why she didn't sound more enthusiastic. "Now all I gotta do is finish the article."

Constables Nakano and Wethers were walking up the sidewalk towards them. Mitch had chosen Nakano as the focus of this article, and he was relieved to see that she seemed her usual no-nonsense self that morning. Not that he was used to doing this kind of thing, but he guessed that if she'd been fussed or flattered, it would probably spoil the article and definitely add a false note to the photos.

Mitch walked forward to shake each of the cops by the hand.

"Good morning, Mr. Delmonaco," said Nakano. "Good morning, Ms. Cody."

"It's Martin, O.K.?" Mitch responded. "And Cody likes to be called just Cody."

"Then it's Adena," Nakano offered with a smile.

"Jack," said Wethers.

Cody remained silent. If Mitch hadn't been feeling charitable, he'd have thought her sullen rather than withdrawn. Still, there was no chance to pursue the matter now.

"Let's head out," Mitch suggested. "We can start by you all letting me treat you to breakfast."

"I'm not hungry," said Cody.

Which was when Mitch realized that there was something seriously wrong. Breakfast was Cody's favorite meal. "Coffee, at least?" he offered.

"That would be very welcome," Adena smoothly replied. "Jack and I were working the late shift until two days ago. I'm still jet-lagged."

The four of them walked off down the sidewalk, with Mitch and Adena taking the lead, and Mitch lighting a smoke. He asked, "Did your P.R. unit lay down any rules I should know about?"

"Nothing that you and I hadn't already discussed. They're grateful for this opportunity, Mr. Delmonaco." She corrected herself. "Martin."

He grinned at her, and the day began. After coffee – that segued into breakfast, after all – the four of them walked the streets together, Adena and Jack taking the opportunity to greet and talk with various residents.

Mitch ended up rather impressed by Adena. She was competent and caring, and made for an ideal 'public face' for the police. The two of them talked throughout the day, with Wethers paying attention and occasionally interjecting his thoughts, or passing on his assessment when Adena downplayed her own contributions.

Cody remained withdrawn, and never really connected with any of them. But she did her job thoroughly enough, and took what Mitch thought would be some great photos of Adena and Jack on duty, or posing with unassuming confidence in the urban locations that comprised their beat.

In the early afternoon Adena and Jack answered a call regarding a domestic dispute, and ended up arresting both the man and the woman involved. Mitch and Cody were given a tour of the police station with

Adena, while Jack booked the arrestees.

The four of them attended a schoolboy rugby league match as the afternoon lengthened into evening. Adena and Jack sorted out an off-field tussle. Then they severely embarrassed some boys and girls by catching them hidden away behind the sheds smoking dope, but let them off with a lecture and a stern warning.

All in all it made for a picturesque day, thought Mitch.

"That's because you didn't see the paperwork side of things," Adena responded, somewhat severely.

They had ended up back near the café in which they'd started that morning. "One more for the road?" Mitch suggested. "Coffee, I mean, of course."

"Are we done?" Cody asked. "'cos I've gotta go. Thank you, both," she added, barely even glancing at Adena and Jack. And she was off striding down the street towards her car before Mitch could say anything. He watched her leave with some frustration, having hoped she'd stay at least long enough for him to get to the bottom of whatever was bothering her.

"I'd better get on as well," Jack said. "Thank you for the day. I hope you got what you wanted, Martin." He shook Mitch's hand, before heading off in a different direction.

That left Mitch and Adena. They settled at an outdoor table, and Mitch ordered coffee while Adena ordered tea. Mitch lit up a cigarette, and they sat there quietly for a while.

Eventually Mitch said, "I'm exhausted. How do you stay on your feet all day?"

"Years of practice, very expensive shoes, and a truckload of bull-headed determination."

He smiled at her, and then swooped in for the kill. "You only did this as a way of finding out more about me, right?"

She returned his smile a little wryly, and only took a moment before replying in reasonable tones, "It's not that I think you're one of the bad guys, Mr. Delmonaco, but I don't know *who* you are. I'm sure you realize that makes me feel as … as curious as you would, if the tables were turned."

"Yeah, I get it. Look, we've both been on-duty today. Do you wanna spend some time with me off-duty as well?"

She didn't say anything, but she looked rather doubtful.

"I don't mean anything inappropriate," Mitch reassured her. "I'm gay, for a start – but that's not the point."

"Don't worry, I didn't misunderstand," she said. "The point is that you think we can be friends."

"Good, yeah. So, I'm catching a movie with a friend tonight. Do you want to come along?"

Adena tilted her head to indicate 'maybe'. "It has been a long day. But what's the movie?"

"Don't know yet. I'll want something American, he'll respectfully suggest something Australian. Last time we compromised on a late late session of Baz Luhrmann's *Romeo and Juliet*."

Adena laughed, but shook her head. "I don't think I'll intrude."

"You won't be intruding. He's 'just' a friend, too. I bet you'll wanna come if I tell you who he is …" Mitch left a significant pause before announcing, "Rory Pierce."

"Who?"

Mitch sat back in his chair feeling rocked. "God, I'm already used to people treating him like the Second Coming. I forgot there'd be somebody somewhere who's never heard of him."

"So who is he?" Adena prompted, with only mild curiosity.

"A minor celebrity, a major hunk. Cody's nuts about him. An architect by day, a party animal by night, but really just a regular guy."

"He sounds awful, Martin."

Mitch blanked in surprise for a moment – and then found himself offering the truth. He rarely felt that vulnerable. "Actually, he's quite beautiful. Inside and out." Had he ever even said the word 'beautiful' out loud before? "He doesn't let all the adulation get to him. Cody has surprisingly good taste."

Adena smiled, and started getting ready to leave as she spoke. "Then I'll gracefully withdraw and leave him to someone who appreciates him. I have some shopping to do. Goodnight, Martin. Thank you again for today."

"No, thank *you*. Goodnight!" Feeling somewhat dazed, Mitch watched as Adena walked away in the direction of the local grocery store. Then after a moment Mitch picked up the check and pulled out his wallet.

Cody had gone straight home, and now sat cross-legged on the whitewashed floor of her studio. Her back was to the photos of Rory. She wasn't looking out the window. She wasn't looking outwards at all. If there had been anyone to look at her, all they would have seen on her face was the barest hint of a soul-deep strain. A strain that was quickly reaching breaking point.

Mitch started walking home from the local stores as the twilight was darkening into night. He noticed that there was some vaguely familiar musclebound guy loitering near a car that was parked just ahead, but he didn't think much of it. Until he drew near and the big guy stepped into the center of the sidewalk, apparently wanting to stop him or talk to him – For a moment, Mitch thought of muggings, even though they were right out in the open – Then Mitch glimpsed someone definitely familiar sitting in the back seat.

He approached warily and the big guy held open the front passenger door for him, effectively blocking his way past. Mitch wasn't stupid enough to just get in. He kept what distance he could, and bent down far enough to look in through the side window and confirm for himself who it was in the back. And of course it was John Bricca. Mitch stared at him.

"Mr. Delmonaco, please," said Bricca. "We have something to discuss. In privacy, if you wouldn't mind."

Mitch straightened up. He didn't like it, but he knew his curiosity would outweigh any other considerations. He dropped his cigarette butt, and stepped on it to extinguish the ember. Then he looked at the guy who was obviously a driver and bodyguard and who knew what else. "Alright, I'll get in," Mitch said to Bricca, "if *he* stays out."

"Of course."

Well, thought Mitch. Honor among thieves, and all that. He slid into the front passenger seat, and let the bodyguard close the door. The fact that Bricca was sitting directly behind him put his hackles up, so Mitch twisted around to his left so he could keep his eyes on both Bricca and the thug who worked for him. Otherwise, Mitch played it cool and remained silent.

Bricca let a long moment pass before continuing. "We both know what this is about, Mr. Delmonaco, so I'll get to the point. If you turn your attention elsewhere, I'll make it worth your while. If you don't –"

The threat was left hanging, and Mitch didn't bother waiting for him to complete it. "Damn it," Mitch equally complained. "There I was hoping to take this opportunity to interview you, but you just wanna bully me."

"And I thought you Yanks didn't get sarcastic."

"Oh, we're both full of surprises today."

"I'll make it real simple for you," Bricca continued in the same urbane tones. "Take the money, or I'll take your life."

"Jeez, let me think about that."

Bricca said, "You wanna self-destruct, fine. That would suit me perfectly."

Mitch didn't respond. For some reason, he felt … flummoxed. He wondered rather vaguely if Bricca would be prepared to have him killed right there and then, on a suburban street when anyone might walk past – and concluded that if the bodyguard had a gun with a silencer, it was perfectly possible, and they would just drive off with him in the passenger seat and dump him somewhere out of the way.

"There's an envelope in the glove box," said Bricca. "Take it."

Mitch found himself acting as if on autopilot. He opened up the glove compartment, and retrieved a rather bulky envelope. Rather than be subtle about it, he unfastened the flap on the envelope, and drew out a bundle of twenty, fifty and one-hundred dollar bills – Australian, of course. And there was still plenty more in the envelope.

Mitch recovered his voice. "You call this real money? God, I still can't get over the colors of it. It's like Monopoly money. And then there's this see-through bit. What the hell is that about … ?"

"Take it," said Bricca. "And don't let me catch you sniffing around anymore."

"It's hardly even a real bribe," Mitch babbled on. "You should come to New York sometime, Mr. Bricca, we have real crime in New York."

"If you can make it there, you can make it anywhere – right?"

"Right." He shrugged. "Well, what the hell, I'll be going home soon."

And Mitch opened the door and climbed out of the car. The envelope was in his hand. He felt … oddly dazed. He couldn't even tell anymore whether he was being stupid or smart, but he supposed at least he wasn't being killed. The bodyguard got out of his way, and Mitch walked off, not acknowledging either Bricca or the other man. And of course they let him go, having won their point.

Mitch didn't see it, but Bricca was sitting there looking smug. "That was easy," he remarked.

And none of the three men saw her, but Adena Nakano was on the sidewalk on the far side of the street, with two bags of groceries hanging from her hands. She'd seen the exchange of money, and she was horrified.

There seemed nothing she could do immediately, so she simply watched as Martin headed for his house, and Bricca was driven away. She read the car's number plate, and repeated it to herself three or four times for the sake of remembering it. Within moments she was alone again, and the night began to draw in.

Mitch walked down the sidewalk and turned in through the gate to his courtyard. He was still carrying the envelope. He was still numb. He didn't even feel anything when he saw that Rory was sitting on his front steps waiting for him, stroking the stray cat which was curled up in his lap.

"Hello, Martin. How was your day?"

Mitch nodded at the pleasantry, but couldn't muster a response. He unlocked the front door – he didn't fumble with the key at all – and Rory followed him inside, the cat still in his arms.

Mitch went through to the kitchen and sat down. He put the envelope of money on the table in front of him, and stared at it. He suspected he'd just been really unaccountably stupid – but had he had any choice? It occurred to him that he wasn't smoking, and he thought rather vaguely that at least he could do something about that.

After a moment, Rory let the cat jump down to the floor, and started to make a pot of coffee. "Martin," he said, while efficiently bustling around the kitchen.

"Yeah?" was all that Mitch managed.

"Martin, I was wondering how Cody is. She seemed a bit … unhappy after the photo-shoot."

"Uh, yeah. She's O.K."

Rory stilled for a moment and looked across at him. "You're sure she's O.K.? I'm glad."

Mitch rubbed at his face with both hands as if he were just waking up.

He thought again about the question. "Actually, she's been a bit quiet today. Is there a problem?"

Rory drew breath to answer –

But that was when somebody pounded on the front door. *Thud, thud, thud.*

The cat dashed away in fright. Mitch looked up, frowning, suddenly alert. He did not move. He did not propose to go answer the door. Rory was watching him, shifting from startled to perplexed.

A moment later the door swung open – crashed bang into the wall – and somebody stormed inside. Mitch stood up to face his fate.

"*Martin*! Mr. Delmonaco!"

Mitch sagged in relief. It was Adena Nakano's voice. He sat back down again as Adena strode into the kitchen, and dropped his head into his hands to avoid her glare. He tried not to think too much about how stunned Rory must be to have this uniformed cop righteously rip into Mitch.

"What the hell kind of game are you playing? You two-faced son of a bitch. I can't believe I let you dupe me. You've been one of the bad guys all along, haven't you? – *Haven't you?*"

"I can explain," he said rather weakly.

"You can *explain* taking money from that man?"

"Well, maybe not that." Mitch sighed, and sat up again, just far enough to face her. "I can explain the rest. Adena. Please sit down."

She didn't sit. But she did remain standing there, with arms folded across her chest, and she did remain silent, giving him the chance to speak.

Mitch glanced at Rory, who was still in the kitchen watching all this with wary concern, a dish towel scrunched in one hand. Then Mitch looked back at Adena. He knew that Rory and Adena were good people and for whatever reason they were prepared to be his friends. It had been stupid to take the money, but somehow that now made it very clear to him that it would be smart to finally tell his friends the truth.

"I *am* a journalist," Mitch said, "I *am* a U.S. citizen, I work for the *New York Times*. But I'm not using my real name – which is Mitch Rebecki."

"Why?"

"I was writing a series of stories on a bad guy. I guess I started hitting too close to home. He started threatening me – not enough for the cops to be able to do much about it, but enough for … Well, Tom Lewis, my editor, is

Eva's cousin. He sent me to work down here until it's safe to go home again."

Rory came over, bearing three mugs of coffee. He put them down on the table, and then sat beside Mitch. He shifted two of the coffees a bit closer so they were within reach, and said, "Hello, Mitch."

Mitch exchanged a friendly look with the man, grateful for such immediate acceptance. He finally shakily reached for his cigarettes, and lit one up. Then he said, "I'm sorry, O.K.? I have to apologize to both of you, and I'll tell Cody, apologize to her. All I can say is, it seemed like a good idea at the time. Adena, I'm one of the good guys."

She still wasn't entirely convinced.

"Adena, I got my passport for Martin Delmonaco through the F.B.I., and they wouldn't have done that if I wasn't on the right side."

"Mr. Rebecki. You just took what looks to be a rather large bribe."

"Yes, I did," he said.

Rory cast a rather startled glance at the envelope that had sat untouched on the table all this while. But then he looked back at Mitch as if he knew there'd be a reason for that as well.

Which made it harder to admit, "I don't know what I was thinking. I wasn't thinking at all. Or maybe I was thinking this isn't my life, not my real life, this isn't real money, he's not a real criminal …"

Adena was unimpressed. "Is that meant to be an explanation?"

"He threatened my life," Mitch asserted rather weakly, "though I have to admit I wasn't sure how seriously to take that."

Adena merely gusted out an impatient sigh.

Mitch looked up at her, truly regretful, and knowing he was in dire need of her help. "How do I make it right?"

She considered him for a long moment, hard-faced. But then at last she said, "I'll make a phone call."

Adena wouldn't say who she'd called, and apparently didn't think it advisable that they discuss Mitch's situation any further until whoever-it-was arrived. And so the three of them sat around the table in silence, drinking coffee, lost in their own thoughts. Mitch's main comfort was that Rory was still there, and seemed by far the least troubled of the three.

At last there was a knock at the front door and Adena went to answer it.

Mitch and Rory exchanged a worried yet curious glance. There was a long pause, though if Adena was talking with whoever-it-was, they were very quiet about it. Then Adena finally came back through to the dining room, followed by a deadly serious man in a black suit, white shirt, black tie and dark sunglasses.

Mitch took one look at him, and erupted in hysterical laughter. "You've got Men in Black here? That's an urban myth! That's an *X-Files* episode – and a comedy one, at that! For God's sake, get serious."

But Adena and Rory were taking the situation very seriously indeed. Rory stayed where he was, sitting next to Mitch, but seemed profoundly wary.

The Man in Black addressed Mitch directly. "Mr. Rebecki, my people are already working on bringing down John Bricca and his colleagues. You can be part of the team, or you can keep playing the lone crusader. Either option comes at a price."

"Who the hell are you?" Mitch asked.

"That's strictly need-to-know, Mr. Rebecki. We don't want a repeat of the situation in New York. We don't want another one of your cats killed."

Mitch gaped in shock at that. He hadn't told anyone here in Australia about Pulitzer. He supposed that Tom would have told Eva – but in any case, it meant that the black-suited man was well-informed.

Once he'd seen that sink in, the man continued, "You're not a team player, Mr. Rebecki."

Mitch was surprised to find that that stung. "And you *are*?" he retorted. "Jeez … I'm an arrogant Yank, what's your excuse?"

"If you're prepared to help, we won't pursue the matter of you accepting the bribe."

"You mean, you won't press charges?"

The black-suited man replied, utterly deadpan, "Something like that."

Well. Mitch didn't have much choice, though he felt horribly resentful. "Alright … But don't be trying to tell me my job has no redeeming value, team player or not."

There was no response. They were all waiting on him.

"Alright, alright," he grumbled. "What do you want me to do?"

Adena had set up a video camera on a tripod to record Mitch while he was being interviewed by the Man in Black – who was seated across the table from Mitch, but deliberately stayed out of camera range. Rory had made them all more coffee, and was otherwise keeping quietly out of the way.

Mitch had finally wound to the end of his tale. "And Bricca said, 'There's an envelope in the glove compartment.' He said I should take it."

The black-suited man asked, "Do you have that money with you now?"

Mitch held up the envelope in front of the video camera, and opened it far enough so that a viewer could see the money. "It's all here, I've hardly even touched it."

"Constable, please bag that."

Adena came over with a clear plastic evidence bag and held it open for him. Mitch dropped in the envelope with its contents, and then Adena sealed and marked the bag – all in front of the camera, so there was a clear chain of possession of the evidence.

"Is there anything else, Mr. Rebecki?"

"No. He just said again that I should mind my own business. I don't know if they would have killed me then and there, but I got the impression it would only be a matter of time if I didn't cooperate."

"Thank you. Constable, if you'd take a seat, I'll take a statement from you as well."

Mitch stood up at last, feeling a sense of relief, and then it was Adena's turn to sit in the chair. Mitch went to stand beside Rory, and seeing as they hadn't been told to make themselves scarce, they watched the interview begin.

"Constable Nakano, if you could formally identify yourself, and then tell me about when you first became aware of this situation …"

It was almost midnight before they were done. Mitch and Rory were sitting at the table, their heads propped on their hands. Rory was looking exhausted, though still untarnished. Mitch hated to think how he himself looked. The cat finally dared to wander back in, and then leaped up onto Rory's lap for comfort.

Finally Mitch heard the front door close, and Adena walked back in.

"Thank God that's over," said Mitch.

"For now," replied Adena.

"Oh yeah, until the part where Bricca tries to kill me."

Adena looked at him with mingled sympathy and impatience. "Maybe you shouldn't be alone tonight."

"I'll stay," Rory offered promptly.

But Adena continued, "Maybe you shouldn't be here tonight. Don't go emigrating again, but it might be wise to change your routine, and spend your time with as many people as you can."

Rory turned to Mitch and said, "Come to my place for the night, then."

"What's left of it," Mitch said tiredly. "The night, I mean. O.K., thanks." At this point Mitch was feeling distinctly fond. "Adena, did I get around to formally introducing you to the one and only Rory Pierce … ?"

"No, I guess you didn't."

But Adena was still uninterested, and Rory's smile was so tired as to be little better than polite, so Mitch let the matter be.

Mitch hadn't been to Rory's before. He was surprised to discover that Rory lived in an apartment rather than a house, though it was one of only four apartments in a relatively compact building. The place was modern in design, and relatively new. Mitch was already familiar enough with Rory's style to recognize his work in the enormous floor-length windows punctuating the walls; he liked that Rory lived and worked in places he'd designed himself.

Inside, the apartment was spacious, with a feeling that everything had been done properly. There'd been no cutting of corners; there were no narrow hallways or odd leftover spaces. The décor was stylish but minimalist, in soothing colors. The outside wall of the main room was one enormous window with two wide, carpeted steps running along its foot, and a few cushions piled at one corner as if the steps were used as a window seat. Mitch was impressed despite his exhaustion.

Rory led him further in, and intoned, "Welcome to my ostentatious abode."

"It's great," said Mitch. He was used to the deadpan Australian humor by now, but he chose to take Rory's words at face value. "And if it's really ostentatious I need a new dictionary."

When Mitch turned around he noticed that one wall contained nothing but a framed wedding photo of Rory and Eva, which was rather unexpected. He looked at Rory in curiosity.

Rory seemed a little saddened, a little chagrined. "I should take that down. You know, I wanted the marriage to work – but I wasn't surprised when it didn't."

Mitch considered him. There was no denying his own curiosity about this man. Mitch knew he was as intrigued as anyone.

Rory finally said into the silence, "I'm not in love with her anymore, Mitch. But she mattered to me. Very much."

"I get that," Mitch said with a nod.

There was a moment in which, oddly enough, Mitch felt that Rory was on the brink of propositioning him. Mitch put it down to his own overactive imagination. The vibe was there, Mitch felt, but no doubt it was just the Yank misinterpreting the Australian.

Rory sighed, and ran a hand back over his hair. "It's late," he remarked, "and you've been through a lot tonight." He offered a surprisingly shaky smile. "We've both got things on our mind. I'm worried about –"

He stopped, and left a pause that Mitch didn't fill.

Eventually Rory continued, "Come on, the guest room is through here."

Nine

Rory dropped Mitch at the *Herald* offices the next morning, and then powered off in his MG. Once Mitch had made an appearance in the newsroom, he went down to Cody's office to wait for her to arrive. He sat in her chair with his feet up on the desk, pensively thinking though he hardly knew about what. He was staring at her wall of photos, which was natural enough as they provided the only life in the room. He might even have been staring at one of the photos of Rory, but he was too lost in thought to really see it. His hands were still.

Suddenly Cody burst in. "Where the hell have you been? I waited outside your place for ages this morning, I was late for work, I just got an earful from Eva –"

"I'm sorry," he said, feeling a stab of chagrin. He swung his feet down to the floor, and sat up straighter. "I should have called."

"Damn right you should have. So, where were you?"

"I was at Rory's. Cody, I really –"

"*What?!*"

He grimaced. "Don't leap to conclusions, O.K.? I have to tell you – something kind of dramatic happened last night."

"Dramatic?! Is that what you call it? How *could* you?"

Cody had been restlessly pacing, partly because she was angry, of course, but no doubt partly because Mitch was sitting in her chair. Now she hauled her camera out, and he knew how that would go. Mitch got to his feet, and snapped, "Don't hide behind that thing. Just put it down, and look at me. I've got something to tell you."

"You *bastard*! I don't want to *look* at you!"

"Hey, you know, if you really want him, I don't think he'd object. All you gotta do is be his friend. He's as lonely as the rest of us."

"I *don't* want him," she cried. "Don't you get it?! *I don't want him!*"

They were glaring at each other now. Well. There was no point in Mitch trying to tell her about his real identity under the circumstances, and he couldn't see how to defuse the situation, so eventually he simply stalked out.

As far as Cody was concerned, the best thing about the darkroom was that it doubled as a bunker. She was sitting on a bench there, huddled up in her misery. She was alone. But that was what it always came down to, wasn't it? She was always and forever alone. And in fact there were plenty of times she liked it that way.

Time passed.

Eventually someone tried to intrude, of course. The revolving airlock – which should have been called a lightlock, Cody mused – was designed to always be open. Cody had, however, jammed wooden wedges in at each side of the doorway so the thing couldn't be spun back around. There was a frustrated thumping that resounded hollowly through the small space.

In contrast, Eva's voice sounded sharp. "Cody! Open the door!" A moment, before she continued irritably, "Come on, Cody – you really don't want to miss another deadline."

Cody remained silent, and didn't stir. She felt too dull to respond at all.

"Cody, *please* ..." Eva continued, her tones a little more concerned than Cody would have expected. Though she was soon back to simple anger. "Oh, damn it, Cody, come on! Open the door!"

Nothing. Cody had nothing.

Eva gave the door one last *thump*, and then her footsteps tap-tapped away across Cody's office and out the door.

Alone again. Cody sighed. Naturally.

At last it was election day for the local council – and on a Saturday, which apparently was standard practice in Australia. Mitch would have been ridiculously grateful that it would soon be over, if only he weren't too tired and distracted to feel anything much at all.

He and Cody were currently covering a polling booth located at a school. Cody was even more disgruntled and distant than Mitch himself. And that was saying something, as Mitch – to his own surprise – seemed to have quit smoking, and the withdrawal symptoms were hellish. The day itself was as restless as Mitch and Cody combined. Posters were being blown about in a gusty wind, and it seemed even regular people were being driven to distraction.

Mitch finished interviewing a couple of voters and headed back to where

Cody was hanging around. "Looks like the mayor will win by a landslide," he remarked. "I bet it'd be different if I could publish the whole story."

There was no response from Cody.

"Cody," Mitch said for the tenth time, "I'm sorry about this undercover business. I could have told my friends who I am. I should have."

"Do you really think I care?"

Mitch looked at her hard for a moment. She might not care about Mitch, but there was someone else she definitely cared about, and it was obviously making her miserable. "Cody, this thing you've got for Rory –"

"Thing?" she said with sharp sarcasm. "What thing? I don't have a thing."

"Damn it – either go *do* something with him, or find somebody else to get passionate about. Looks like it's eating you alive right now."

"I don't know you, Martin Delmonaco or whatever the fuck your name is – and you sure as hell don't know me. This has nothing to do with him! Leave me alone."

Roundly defeated on all counts, Mitch sighed and wandered off.

At least Adena was still talking to him. She came round to Mitch's place that evening to help him write up a full statement. They'd ordered pizza, and were now sitting at the table with Mitch's laptop open in front of them. A new document glowed emptily at him. The cat was curled up peacefully on the seat of the chair where Rory usually sat. Rather than start typing, Mitch reached to run a hand round the cat's back, not stroking so much as seeking reassurance.

"You're a writer," Adena said. "What's the problem? Just put it in your own words."

"What *are* my own words?" Mitch asked, with an edge of humor. "This isn't like writing an article."

"For heaven's sake, just start typing! Start with why you began to suspect that Knight Construction is up to no good."

Mitch looked at her. "Your Man in Black ain't gonna give a damn about the building company side of things. He just wants the large-scale organized crime stuff, right?"

"If they don't follow up these other details," she said, "I will."

He was just about to set his hands to the keyboard when the doorbell rang – which must be the pizza, though Mitch was more grateful for the interruption. "Oh, thank God."

But Adena stood up, and pinned him to his chair with a look. "I'll get that. You start typing. I'll let you have a slice of pizza once you've finished the first paragraph."

"Tyrant!" he cried after her.

Adena just laughed.

Cody locked herself in the darkroom again, once the working day had ended and pretenses no longer needed to be maintained. She couldn't get warm, though. She was sitting curled up on a bench, arms wrapped around herself, shivering. She'd turned on the red light even though she wasn't processing, but the color only provided the illusion of warmth. She was cold and alone.

There was nothing else. There was nothing.

Adena was reading Mitch's report on the laptop. He sat beside her, waiting for queries or requests for more detail, different phrasing. He'd grabbed an apple from the fruit bowl and now passed it from one hand to the other, exploring its shape and texture, simply to have something to do. Adena seemed to find this distracting. The cat had vanished.

"For God's sake," Adena finally said. "Have a cigarette if you want one; don't mind me."

"I don't want one," Mitch replied. "I don't want one."

Adena cast him a dubious look, then turned back to the report. "This is good. Very thorough. Have you got anything else to prove the reselling of the building materials that Mr. Valeri donated?"

"No, I haven't had a chance to follow that up yet. At the moment it's just suspicions."

Adena nodded thoughtfully, and continued reading.

Eva was alone in her office, reading through the last of that day's stories and making any necessary changes. It was late, and the main room below her had been empty long enough that the lights above it – controlled by a motion detector – had dimmed. It felt as if Eva was the only person in the whole building. Sensing a presence, though, Eva looked up – and was startled to see Cody at one edge of the doorway.

Cody slowly slipped inside the office, but kept her distance as if she didn't appreciate the stark light. Something was obviously very wrong. She seemed distracted and distraught. Eva lit a cigarette and considered her carefully.

Eventually Cody said, "I had him. Once. Well, twice actually, one night. After the photo-shoot."

Of course. Eva understood now. She left a silence while they both thought about Rory Pierce. Eventually Eva said, "You poor girl."

"There's no reaching him, is there? And even if you reach him, there's no keeping him."

"No."

"I never got why you left him."

No one got it, of course, and Eva hadn't bothered trying to illuminate anyone else. "Do you understand now? He's too much for a mere mortal to bear up close. You stand beside him, inevitably you're compared to him – no one should suffer that. He can't help it, he is what he is. But I finally decided to make survival a priority."

Cody said with wistful sincerity, "Poor Rory." She lost herself in contemplation for a while, but then shook herself back to the present. "I do understand, but that's not it for me."

"Isn't it?"

"This isn't about him," Cody continued. "Martin was right – Mitch. It would be easy if it was. Way easier than I thought. But it isn't."

And with a wan smile Cody drifted out the door. Eva was left frowning after her.

Adena and Mitch were waiting in her car across the street from Valeri's offices. It was late, but the warmth of the day hadn't dissipated, and Mitch had worn a jacket mostly so that he could shove his hands into the pockets in an effort to keep them still. This not smoking thing was a nightmare, especially when there was nothing to distract him.

Eventually Valeri drove up in a utility vehicle – the sort that was a hybrid of a car and a flat-bed truck. Australians loved the misbegotten thing, apparently, though of course 'utility vehicle' was too long a name so in typical laconic fashion they called it a 'ute'.

The three of them congregated at the front door of the offices, which Valeri unlocked. He was fighting an enormous yawn, and seemed somewhat disgruntled. "This really couldn't wait for business hours?"

"Hey," Mitch said, "you wanted me to do something about Knight Construction, and that's what I'm doing."

They made their way inside. Valeri switched on a minimal number of lights.

"I'm sorry, Mr. Valeri," Adena said, somewhat more diplomatically, "but we want to keep this as discreet as possible for as long as we can."

After a moment, Valeri huffed an ironic laugh, and offered her a small smile. "Yeah, I can't really blame you for that."

"The goods you donated to the council project, that you suspect they resold – I need to see all the records relating to that."

Valeri was obviously tired and feeling a bit put-upon, but he was a decent guy. He heaved a sigh and headed for the filing cabinets.

Cody had finally gone home. She was sitting curled up on the floor in the main room of her apartment, alone except for the half-empty bottle of vodka beside her. She didn't even have her camera with her – she'd left it on the table with her bag and keys. Her mobile phone had rung a few times, but she'd ignored it. She felt bare. Completely exposed. She was still trembling with cold. Everything good had drained away as if it had hardly even existed in the first place, and she was left with … nothing.

Eventually she got up, and sluggishly searched for the nearest photo of Rory. Then she found a marker pen, and scrawled a note on the back of the photo. 'It's not about him.' She left it all where it was – but at the last moment she picked up the camera in one hand, and then she headed out the front door.

Instead of turning right for the lift, she turned left and walked along a short corridor. One of the neighbors – Eric? – said hello, and seemed to want to talk, to question her, but she kept going, pushing past him, and reached the door to the stairwell.

She was on the top floor so there was only one flight of stairs to the roof.

She emerged into night air so cold that it struck through to her marrow. But she wouldn't be cold much longer.

She walked to the parapet at the edge of the roof, and glanced down to the street far below. Horror crawled through her belly, undermining her resolve for a moment, so instead she fixed her gaze on the distant place where the city lights vanished into the darkness, and she took a deep calming breath. She lifted the camera and carefully took a photo of what she could see, and then she put the camera down on the parapet. She wouldn't need it anymore. She didn't need it. She took another breath. Then gracefully she lifted her arms to either side ... closed her eyes ... and let herself topple slowly forward.

Cody disappeared from view.

There was a still moment in which there was nothing but the city lights and the horizon and the dark sky above.

Then there was a *thud* and a squeal of brakes from the street below, a cry from a pedestrian, shocked voices. But that was all quite muted, as if it were occurring a long way away, and the empty view remained, a little cold but also peaceful.

Ten

Eva was standing alone in the middle of Cody's office, shaking despite her attempts to hold herself together. Ash fell from her cigarette. She took a drag on it, frantic for the comfort of nicotine. She glared at the photos of Rory that Cody had pinned to the wall. There were none from that last photo-shoot of course. Eva could see now that was when it had all gone so very wrong. She had thought she understood, but she hadn't. She'd thought Cody was far more resilient than Eva herself. She'd never been sorrier to be wrong.

Eventually Mitch walked in. He looked pale and thoroughly shaken, but also dazed as if the news was only just starting to really hit home. After a searching look around the office, he fixed on Eva as if desperate for a comforting word.

But she was feeling far too bitter and angry to offer him any such thing. "I suppose suicides aren't as tragic here as in the States."

Mitch flinched, doubly hurt.

"Is this real enough for you?" Eva cried.

A fraught moment passed.

"You were meant to look after her," she insisted in a somewhat steadier voice. "You were meant to cut him down to size for her."

Apparently Mitch had nothing to plead in his defense. They each stood there alone, stranded by shock and grief.

The funeral took place on a raw, restless day, the mourners buffeted by the wind and occasional squalls of rain. That was appropriate, Mitch thought. The cemetery was on a bare grassy headland so high it felt as if it were thrust halfway up to the sky. The ocean surged at the foot of the cliffs, so far below. The setting was more dramatic than lovely. That was appropriate, too. Not that anything could be right about any of this, but if it had to be so then this was the place. He didn't know how long it would take Cody to find peace there, but until she did she might at least feel that she belonged.

Mitch wondered if Cody would have been surprised by the number of mourners. There was a good-sized gathering of people at the graveside service, most dressed somberly but with a few defiant and entirely appropriate splashes of color. The wind seemed to strip everyone to essentials; hats and umbrellas were impossible to manage, so they all stood exposed to the elements.

Eva was there, of course, standing next to Mitch at the graveside. They were both wearing dark sunglasses. Eva had left her long red hair loose for the first time that Mitch had seen. It was blown about wildly, occasionally whipping against Mitch's face.

Adena was standing behind Mitch, serious and sober in her dress uniform.

Rory was also there, of course. Mitch was conscious of him standing at the back of the group, almost separate from it, keeping out of the way. He wasn't wearing sunglasses, though, or trying to hide or protect himself. He looked drained, but also withdrawn, as if he were too tactful to impose his own grief on anybody else under such difficult circumstances.

There were other faces that Mitch recognized from the newspaper office. A bewildered old man stood beside the priest with tears in his eyes – Eva told Mitch this was Cody's grandfather. There was no other family.

The coffin was lowered and the brief service ended. Cody's grandfather walked away with the priest, and the others began to follow them. The last mourners left were Mitch, Eva and Rory – though Rory still kept his distance. Then Eva turned, threw a furious glare at Rory, and stalked away.

Mitch lit a cigarette, his first for a while, and felt the harsh power of it flay him from inside. Rory approached, and offered a comforting grasp of his shoulder. The gesture could have become a hug, if Mitch had wanted it. But he didn't.

Mitch turned and walked away as well.

That night Rory sat with his back against the enormous window in his living room, sitting on the steps without the comfort of a cushion. The room was dark, which made Rory all the more conscious of the city lights behind him, each one cold and yet signifying the warmth of a human life. He couldn't bear to look at them, remembering too vividly those moments in which he and Cody had been gazing out across just such a view from her apartment, and she had turned to him and finally kissed him.

Is this really a good idea?

He was still in the same clothes he'd worn to the funeral that day, as if shedding them would somehow mean the very last farewell. It was all the harder to let go when he knew he should have taken better care right from the start.

There was a loud knock at the door. Rory didn't do more than sit up and lean his elbows on his knees. Perhaps he'd been missed from the post-funeral reception after all.

Another knock, and then an urgent cry. "Rory! Rory, are you in there? It's Mitch."

A loud rattle as Mitch tried the door handle – and then a surprised silence, and a different quality to the air. Rory didn't remember leaving the door unlocked, but he must have.

A moment later Mitch peered into the room and saw Rory. At which point he turned away – this time only to go back to firmly close and lock the front door. Then he returned.

The two men stared at each other across the endless space of the room. Rory figured he must be able to see Mitch better than Mitch could see him – Rory's eyes were adjusted to the dimness, and Mitch wasn't silhouetted against the window. Mitch seemed a bit wild, but not in a way that made Rory fearful. A tumultuous silence stretched.

Then Mitch harshly declared, "If you think I'm gonna destroy myself over you, you're wrong."

Rory replied very quietly, "I'm glad."

Mitch started walking closer, but slowly, almost as if unable to help himself but fighting the impulse every step of the way.

Finally he was close enough to see Rory properly – and Rory didn't try to hide how upset he was feeling. At which, it seemed that all of Mitch's resentment and guilt and anger was undone.

He reached a hand, which Rory took, and once Rory was standing, Mitch took him into his arms. Rory had never felt so profoundly relieved. They held each other as friends, as an equal pair of all-too-fallible human beings.

Eventually Mitch eased back a little, without entirely letting Rory go, and offered, "She said it wasn't about you."

"I know," he replied, his throat scratchy with disuse. "But it's hard not to feel … complicit."

"You're not responsible for me, O.K.?"

"I know. You're responsible for you." Rory looked very directly at Mitch, and said, "So don't destroy yourself over Bricca, either. Alright?"

Mitch had to drop his head and hide a little to think about that. But eventually he said, "Alright."

"Good," said Rory. "Then for God's sake, come to bed with me."

Mitch lifted his head again and gazed hard at Rory, as if hardly daring to believe. But then at last Mitch was brave enough to lean in and begin a slow, deep, beautiful kiss.

When he was done, Rory took Mitch by the hand and led him to his bedroom.

Mitch half-woke in the small hours needing to move, having been lying too long on one side. Rory was pressed heavily against him, with an arm and a leg flung across him for good measure. Mitch smiled, and tried to shift gently so as not to disturb the man. But Rory half-woke, too, and instinctively followed Mitch as he turned. It seemed they were both in need of a sense of security. Mitch drifted back to sleep with a contented smile on his face.

There would be an inquest into Cody's death, of course, though Mitch thought it seemed pretty clear from the start that the conclusion would be suicide. A neighbor said that he'd seen Cody going up to the roof, but that things had seemed normal – that she'd been in 'one of her moods' but that she'd had her camera with her. Mitch didn't blame him for not going after her. He wouldn't have done so either.

Some people seemed determined to think that Cody had slipped while clambering onto the parapet for the sake of seeking the perfect photograph. Those who knew her better were all too sure that wasn't the case. She'd taken her final shot. Mitch would stare at a copy of it every now and then, gazing into the infinity of the horizon beyond the city lights.

He liked to think he could see a sense of peace there.

It became a habit for Mitch and Rory to drink espresso at the same Oxford

Street café. They were there one day when spring had just changed to summer, sitting outside to enjoy the warm weather, though Mitch was no longer smoking. He hardly even thought about it anymore, and his hands were quiet.

The waiter was channeling Mercutio from the Luhrmann film that day. He wasn't wearing the all-white party outfit but the sheer white shirt, black pants and silver crucifix, along with a mock gun holster of black with white fleurs-de-lis. He looked gorgeous, and his hips slinked when he walked … Not that Mitch thought much about that, either.

Mitch was with Rory, and he was – in his own brusque New York way – happy. As before, the other gay men at the café were staring at Rory, and gossiping about him, but now they also speculated about whether Mitch and Rory were lovers or not. Mitch thought it was probably pretty obvious that they were. They were comfortable enough to tease and flirt with each other in public, and Rory would even camp it up on occasion. Actually Mitch thought it must be pretty hard to miss by now.

Once they'd been served their second coffees, Rory asked, "Are you doing anything tonight? I've got tickets to the premiere of the new James Bond film."

"Really?" Mitch responded. "Wow. They'll give them away to just anybody, huh?"

Rory pouted like an accomplished old roué. "Not at all, darling. One has to be a beautiful celebrity like *moi*."

Mitch couldn't help but laugh. "You'd better keep the second ticket – you'll need somewhere to put your ego for the evening."

"No, my ego floats overhead like a colorful balloon … It's not as weighty as yours, you arrogant Yank."

"Oh yeah, the excess baggage they charged me on the flight over almost bankrupted me."

They were both laughing by now. Mitch picked up his espresso and happened to catch a look of amusement from one of the other customers – and a look of envy, too. *I understand*, Mitch thought. *There are times I even envy myself.*

After a moment, Rory sobered. He pushed his own coffee aside, and leaned in closer to say quietly, "Don't take this the wrong way –" He stopped, and chuckled. "I'm not sure if you should take it the right way, either, for that matter. But you're one-in-a-million to me, Mitch."

"That does it – I'll have so much excess baggage on the way home, I'll need to charter my own airplane." His teasing was gentle, but even so, after another moment Mitch relaxed and matched Rory's sincerity. "What makes me, of all people, one-in-a-million?"

"Lots of dancing," said Rory. "No pedestals."

Mitch understood. They were gazing at each other, briefly lost in their own world, utterly satisfied with each other – and for a moment, perhaps, the café was quiet and the street as well, as everybody else was equally spellbound by this small scrap of true appreciation. Mitch dared to brush Rory's hand with his own.

Then Mitch sat back and the moment broke. The usual café clatter and chatter rose around them, and the traffic sped past. But Mitch was still smiling, and it seemed almost impossible to quit.

They attended the premiere of *Casino Royale* that night, though Mitch might have refused if he'd known they'd be expected to do the red carpet thing. The distance was fairly short from the street curb to the cinema's foyer, but trouble massed to either side. Excitable fans pressed against the barricade on the right, and reporters with microphones and cameras were just as excitable on the left. Not to mention that there were even more fans lining the street. Cops were needed to direct the traffic and keep it all under some kind of control.

Mitch and Rory stood at a distance from all the fuss, taking it in. The local celebrities were dropped by limousines at the end of the red carpet, but some made their way back along the fans, signing autographs and taking photos with them. Mitch didn't know who any of the locals were.

"All these fans," Mitch said to Rory. "They must have come for you, right?"

Rory snorted. "You know very well they're here for Daniel Craig – and, frankly, I suspect he's the only reason you agreed to come as well."

"You see right through me," Mitch agreed ironically. "My motivations are transparent."

Another limousine pulled up outside the cinema, and Mitch and Rory took the opportunity to cross the street. They were obliged to walk past some of the fans that lined the curb. Quite a few of them recognized Rory, and asked for his autograph – or more to the point, Mitch thought, they asked for a moment of his time and attention. Rory was always genuine in response, and was happy to really engage with people, even when Mitch thought the fans were treating him as an object. But that was one of the surprises Rory had given Mitch – the fact that the man could be kind without being patronizing, and honest without leaving himself exposed.

Mitch waited patiently off to one side, and felt amused rather than offended when people looked at him thoughtfully and then dismissed him as nobody of importance. Once Rory was free to move on, the two of them set foot on the red carpet – and then the reporters must have their turn.

Rory posed good-naturedly for a few photos, smiling while the flashes went off. They'd both dressed smartly, as Rory had of course expected this. Mitch waited again, a discreet distance away so he wouldn't be caught in the photos. But despite Mitch's best self-effacing efforts, he was noticed – and Mitch himself recognized the shrill gossip columnist from the official opening of Rory's office building.

"Who's your friend, Rory?" the reporter asked.

Rory cast a smile at Mitch, and beckoned him closer. "Be nice to him, Trevor, he's a journalist, too. This is Martin Delmonaco from the *Herald*. He works for Eva Lewis."

"You and Eva have joint custody of him, do you?"

"Eva and I have many mutual friends."

Rory had already turned to head into the foyer when the reporter attempted a hit below the belt. "Well, you have one fewer now – or so I heard."

Rory turned a stony face to the reporter, rightly heedless of the cameras still going off. Mitch didn't bother hiding his own intense disapproval of this remark – to bring it up now after a few weeks had passed, and Rory might reasonably be considered to be healing, was beyond deplorable. But rather than dignify the remark with a retort, he took Rory's arm and led him inside the cinema. Rory went along with him easily enough.

Mitch found somewhere they could stand off to one side, out of everybody else's way, and out of the line-of-sight from the street. He wanted to soothe Rory, and comfort him – Mitch desperately wanted to hug him. But he still wasn't sure what would be welcome in public, and how far he could go. He shoved his hands in his pockets in order to resist temptation, and he simply stood very close so that they could talk quietly.

Mitch said, "The sooner you accept that all reporters are bastards, the happier you'll be."

Rory almost managed a half-smile. "You're no bastard."

"Well, I bet that bitch wouldn't be, either, if he got to sleep with you."

Reluctant at first, Rory's smile became a slightly brighter thing. The two of them shared an easier moment. Then Rory said, "I'll never forget her, you know. I won't forget Cody."

"I know," Mitch replied. "I won't, either."

And then finally they headed through the foyer, towards the cinema entrance.

There was a semi-official gathering in a nearby bar after the premiere. Mitch and Rory attended, along with a crowd of others – including the reporters, some of whom were already writing, typing or dictating their reactions to the film. The general mood was one of celebration and excitement. Even Mitch felt a bit giddy.

Mitch was sitting at the bar on a stool, leaning forward on his elbows and chatting with a fellow hack on his left. Rory was standing beside him on Mitch's right, but with his back to the bar, also talking with a reporter. Though Mitch and Rory were facing in different directions and involved in different conversations, they were very close to each other, within a hair's breadth of pressing up against each other. Mitch could feel Rory's warmth from his shoulder down to his hip and onto his thigh – and it made him want more.

Mitch's conversation ended, and he signaled to the bartender for another drink. Then, without shifting, he turned his head – that's how close he was – to murmur a detailed proposition in Rory's ear.

Rory almost blushed in reaction, and his eyes widened a little. After a brief falter, though, Rory returned his full attention to the reporter he was conversing with.

"Uh, who's your friend, Rory?" the other guy asked.

"What friend?" Rory lightly replied. "I don't have any friends …"

They got back to Rory's place rather late that night – and it was a Monday, so they both had to work the next day. More accurately, it was already early on Tuesday morning, and they'd barely have a few hours of sleep. But they were both too stirred up to be sensible and forgo the chance to have sex. Mitch, with his writer's pedantry, was beginning to wonder if the act should really be called 'making love'.

It was a very equal and mutual thing. They were active, both eager, and so they rolled to and fro and over and under each other with a sensual energy, neither of them seeking or gaining the upper hand. They kissed like wild things, like they could never quite get enough. There was a beauty in it, and a truth, and the expression on Rory's face when he came was the most exquisite thing Mitch had ever witnessed.

It was making love, of course it was. But Mitch only admitted that in the privacy of his own mind. Because after all, he was in no position to start talking about short-term plans, let alone long-term ones – and he wasn't the kind of guy to even think about 'forever'.

Eleven

Early one morning – even earlier than usual, because Mitch had to go 'home' before he went to work – Mitch was dressing in one of his better suits. It wasn't that the day demanded a good suit, but Mitch only had a certain amount of clothing available at Rory's. The stray American and the stray cat had for all intents and purposes moved into Rory's apartment, but Mitch wasn't quite ready to acknowledge as much, though it meant the occasional inconvenient detour. He wasn't even ready to quit paying rent on the terrace house, even if it had become little more than a token of independence.

Once Mitch was fully dressed, he went to find Rory, who in contrast was wearing nothing but a loose silk robe, and looking like Sensuality personified.

Rory had obviously just put out fresh food for the cat, who was happily scoffing it down. He smiled when Mitch appeared, as he always did, and he asked, "When are you going to name her?"

"How do you know it's a her?"

Rory looked at him, deadpan. "I am not going to discuss the genitalia of cats at this time of day. Not even with you."

Mitch huffed a laugh. "Fine by me. I'll take your word for it. Anyway, I'd better get going."

"What's your rush? Wait, and I'll drive you."

Mitch was grinning happily, but he still had to go. "I can resist anything but temptation."

"That's the idea," Rory brightly agreed.

"No, I've gotta go, the cab will be waiting." Mitch exchanged one more kiss with the man, and then he made himself leave.

The taxi dropped Mitch off by his terrace house. He handed over enough cash to cover the fare and a tip – probably too generous a tip for Australia, but old habits died very hard. As he headed for his front gate, he sorted through his keys for the right one, which he hadn't used for a while. So his head was down. But something caught his eye.

Looking up, Mitch saw John Bricca's driver and bodyguard standing a few feet away on the sidewalk, and Bricca sitting in the back of his car, waiting for Mitch. The morning abruptly soured.

After a moment, Mitch warily approached the car. When he was close enough he leaned down to talk through the open passenger's side window. "What do you want? I thought we were done."

Bricca replied with exaggerated civility. "I'm here to offer you an opportunity, Mr. Delmonaco, and you're giving me attitude."

"I'm a Yank, what do you expect?"

"I expect cleverness and self-interest."

Mitch just stared at the man.

"Would you please get in the car, Mr. Delmonaco?" Bricca asked again in patient tones, as if Mitch were simply being unreasonable.

"Tell me what you want, and then I'll think about it."

"We're going to fly to the Hunter Valley for the day," said Bricca. "Mayor Smithson is going to show you around the winery. You're going to do one of your glossy articles about it. There'll be another envelope waiting for you tonight."

Mitch scoffed a laugh. "Business needs a boost, does it?"

"Actually the vineyard's doing rather well. You can write about what a thriving place it is."

"If you don't need a puff piece, then what is this really about?"

Bricca sighed, as if bored with having to spell things out for the moron. "I have some other business to oversee. I'd like people to think I'm somewhere else today."

"So you need an alibi. Why? You gonna murder somebody? Even I've got to draw a line somewhere, you know."

"I might indeed commit murder if you don't get in the car soon, Mr. Delmonaco."

"Oh yeah," Mitch responded, laying on the sarcasm, "that's the way to get me to cooperate. What guarantee do I have that I'll make it home again?"

"None. Except that I can see you're going to be useful to me, Mr. Delmonaco. For a start, I need you to write this article. Later on, you can do research for me. You can publish or withhold certain information, apparently unconnected with my interests … You'll be very useful."

Mitch gave this a long moment of thought, and then made up his mind. "Alright. But I'd better call my boss. She's expecting me this morning, we have an appraisal meeting with the head honcho at the paper. If I don't turn up, she'll get real mad, she'll move heaven and earth to find me. You don't need that kind of fuss, right?"

Bricca appeared reluctant.

Mitch forged ahead regardless, and pulled out his cell phone. "I'll call her now, and you can listen in, O.K.?"

He straightened up, pressed the third speed-dial number on his phone, and waited while it rang, endeavoring to appear casual and unconcerned.

At the police station, the phone on Adena's desk began ringing – but she wasn't there, and neither was Jack Wethers. One of the other police officers approached –

At the last moment Adena returned, gave the officer a grateful smile, and picked up the handset herself. "Constable Adena Nakano, how can I –"

"Hey, Eva, it's Martin," said a familiar male voice in breezy tones. "No, not that Martin, the Delmonaco Martin."

Adena frowned in confusion, but her mind was already racing to add things up. "Mitch … ?"

"Look, something's come up," Mitch continued in the same tones. "You're gonna have to face the boss without me this morning."

"O.K.," Adena said, as quietly as she could just in case there was anyone near Mitch who might overhear her side of the conversation. "Try to tell me what's happening."

"Yeah, I know – I'm sorry, but I just got an offer to spend the day at the mayor's winery. I can do a great article on it, maybe even a lifestyle piece for the *Times*. But apparently the trip has gotta be today."

Adena's gut sank as she realized the dangerous implications. "Someone's taking you to the Hunter Valley … ? God, is it Bricca?"

"Yeah, that's right. Tell the boss about it. He'll understand."

"I'm on it," Adena promised him. "Hang in there, alright?"

Bricca was getting impatient. "It's time to leave, Mr. Delmonaco."

"I've gotta go," Mitch said into the phone. "I guess we're heading for the airport now, make a full day of it."

Adena urgently replied, "Don't turn off your mobile!"

"Yeah. Gotta go, Eva. I'll call you when I get back tonight."

Mitch ended the call, and then casually slipped the phone into his pocket. He was afraid that Bricca would be smart enough to confiscate the phone, and either leave it behind or turn it off … but Bricca didn't seem to think of doing any of it.

"If you'd get in the car, Mr. Delmonaco."

The driver opened the front passenger door for Mitch, who finally got in. Mitch was worried, but he'd already done what little he could, and he was more concerned now about hiding his reactions from Bricca.

The driver got in, too, and turned the ignition. The car smoothly pulled away from the curb and within moments the street had returned to the usual early morning hush.

After Mitch ended the call, Adena sat there staring at the phone on her desk, thinking things through.

Jack Wethers finally arrived for the day – and as soon as he saw her troubled expression, he drew near. "Problem?"

"I don't know," she said. "Could be something, could be nothing. John Bricca is taking Mitch Rebecki off to the Hunter Valley for the day. Mitch sounded a bit spooked."

"So, what can you do?" Jack asked.

After a moment, she came to a decision. "I'll make a phone call."

She picked up the phone again, and dialed the direct number for the guy Mitch liked to call the Man in Black.

The call was quickly answered. "Yes."

"This is Constable Adena Nakano calling about the Mitch Rebecki case."

"Yes?" he prompted.

"I need you to track his mobile phone for me. Right now, please. We have a situation."

Mitch, Bricca and the driver were silent as the car whisked through the streets. It was still too early for there to be much traffic, but the driver also seemed to be taking back roads and shortcuts. Mitch didn't know Sydney well enough to be able to work out if they were heading for the airport, though he assumed they were.

Abruptly breaking the quiet, Bricca suddenly said to Mitch, "Give me your phone."

Mitch sighed to himself, and passed his cell phone back to Bricca – who switched the phone to speaker, and then hit redial. The beep-beep-beep of a busy signal was the only reply. Mitch was staring ahead through the windshield, tying to appear unconcerned.

After a moment, Bricca hit redial again. This time the call went through, and they heard a ring tone.

Having just hung up again, Adena was startled by her phone ringing. She stared at it, but after another ring she picked up the handset. Her expression was tentative, but her voice was brusque as she answered, "Yes."

"Who's that speaking?" A male voice she didn't recognize, but she had to assume it was Bricca or one of his flunkeys.

Adena replied, "Eva Lewis, the *Herald*. Who's this?" She waited through a brief silence, then asked again in impatient tones, "Who is this?"

Whoever it was hung up, and the dial tone sounded.

Adena put the handset down with a sigh, then looked around for her partner. "Jack, where'd you go? I need you to sit by my phone."

Bricca handed the phone back to Mitch, and Mitch took it. Neither of them said anything. As Mitch slipped it away again, he saw that the phone was still on. He'd been prepared to casually press his thumb against the power button to turn it on again. He wondered what Bricca was thinking … but then for a journalist to have his cell phone off might raise more suspicions than otherwise, and if they were actually going to the Hunter Valley vineyard, then why would Bricca be worried about it being tracked? Mitch frowned, unsure about what this all added up to.

A moment later, the driver turned off the street and took them down a driveway. They were in an industrial area, which was busy on this weekday morning, but Mitch soon saw that they were heading for a warehouse that was set behind other buildings in the block, so it was relatively secluded. In fact, the fences that surrounded it were so high that it wasn't overlooked at all – and the signage announced that it belonged to Knight Construction. Mitch had a very bad feeling about this.

Bricca said, "Come along, Mr. Delmonaco." The driver opened Bricca's door for him, and he strode off towards an open pair of doors as if he owned the place. Which Mitch supposed he did.

The driver opened the passenger door as well, and indicated with a sharp nod that Mitch was expected to follow Bricca. Which Mitch did, feeling wary and confused. The driver brought up the rear, and Mitch didn't feel reassured when another thuggish bodyguard stepped outside the warehouse as he went in, apparently ready to stand watch.

"I thought we were heading for the airport," Mitch said.

"I have some business to take care of first."

"I thought you wanted to be somewhere else."

Bricca cast him a look back over his shoulder. "I'll tell you when I need you to do that much thinking, Mr. Delmonaco."

Mitch followed, curious to find out what was going on, but also wondering at what point he should start panicking. They were still in the midst of suburban Sydney, and it was broad daylight, but he supposed none of that meant Bricca didn't have murder on his mind. On the other hand Bricca had let him call Eva and implicate the mayor in whatever might happen to Mitch that day, so surely Bricca wasn't planning anything too reckless.

Mitch had been confident that he understood the criminal mindset, but right now he wasn't too sure.

Bricca led Mitch and the driver along a corridor past some offices and then into the main warehouse. It was large and echoing, full of building materials and stacked boxes looming up to the roof. The only area that was well-lit was a cleared floor-space into which the three of them walked, so Mitch was aware that there were hiding places all around. His nerve-endings prickled with unease. Waiting out in the open, however, were four other men, all thuggish and all carrying holstered hand-guns.

There were a number of crates also waiting there under the lights. Mitch was close enough to read the shipping and delivery labels – he wasn't sure whether he should worry about that. The crates were addressed to Knight Construction, and originated from Bella Vita Imports & Exports, Bangkok.

One of the thugs said, "We waited for you, Mr. Bricca, just like you said."

"I'm so pleased you can follow such simple orders," Bricca remarked.

Oblivious to the sarcasm, the thug beamed as if he'd been praised. The other thugs remained stoically musclebound.

"Alright," Bricca said. "Open them up."

Mitch frowned, still feeling a mix of worry and curiosity. He really couldn't work out what he was even doing there. Bricca seemed to be ignoring him, and Mitch was all out of clues.

One of the crates was opened. It was full of rather stylish door furniture, with an Italian-sounding brand name. Two of the thugs unpacked it all, stacking it neatly on a nearby pallet. Another crate contained ceramic tiles with an elegant design. It all seemed harmless. But then a third crate was opened. The thugs slipped on rubber gloves and carefully lifted out bolts of beautiful brocade material, along with packets of mothballs. And then clear plastic bags of a fine white powder were taken out. Mitch didn't have much direct experience of such things, but he had to assume that this was heroin or maybe cocaine.

Even as Mitch thought he was starting to understand, Bricca snatched up a bag of heroin and tossed it towards Mitch. He caught it by instinct, in both hands. When he looked up again, he saw that Bricca also had gloves on, while Mitch of course was barehanded.

"You're one of us now," said Bricca.

One of the thugs came over with a fresh plastic bag, and indicated Mitch should drop the heroin into it. He did so, and the package was safely set aside.

"Is *that* was this was about?" Mitch hoped he was still putting on a good front, but underneath there was no denying how queasy he felt. "I was already one of the gang," he scoffed. "You didn't need my fingerprints on this junk to prove it."

Bricca smiled urbanely. "Call it insurance."

"Oh yeah, of course," Mitch muttered in ironic agreement. "You can never be too careful."

The Man in Black had arrived at the police station in an astonishingly short time. He was now standing with Adena at her desk, and they were both watching the tracking device he'd brought with him. There was a motionless red blip on its screen which apparently represented Mitch and his cell phone.

Adena was growing alarmed. "Based on the time Mitch called me, they could have been in this one place for over an hour now. If they're really going to the winery, why aren't they at the airport already?"

Jack hurried over with a computer print-out. He was worried, too. "It's a warehouse, like we thought. But it's owned by what looks like a shell company within a shell company – and it's occupied by Knight Construction."

That decided Adena, at least. "We have to get over there and check it out."

But the black-suited man said, "You're overreacting."

Adena responded fiercely. "Bricca might know Mitch is working with us. Bricca might realize he didn't buy Mitch after all. This Hunter Valley trip could be just a story that gives them time to kill Mitch and dispose of his body before he's even missed."

The Man in Black remained calm – not that he seemed to have any other setting. "That's the worst-case scenario," he said. "Maybe Mr. Rebecki simply left his phone behind at the warehouse."

"Maybe he was forced to," Adena replied.

The two of them stared at each other for a long moment, both stubborn, both determined.

Finally Adena continued, "I'm going there, I'm checking it out. You can back me up if you want to. If you still know what's right and what's wrong. We can decide what to do once we know what's happening. Alright?"

"Alright," he finally agreed.

Within half an hour, Adena had clambered over the fence at the back of the warehouse, picked the lock of a fire escape door, and carefully approached just far enough to be able to see what was going down.

Mitch Rebecki, John Bricca and another man were standing in the only well-lit area of the warehouse, watching while four more men – all armed – unpacked a couple of wooden crates. One of the crates contained bolts of rich brocade, mothballs, and packets of what Adena assumed was an illicit drug. Heroin, probably. The men were carefully stacking the fabric on one pallet, and the heroin on another. Adena slowly leaned a bit further to her right, taking care to remain hidden behind one of the larger boxes towards the rear of the warehouse. Judging from the other empty crates, and the stacks of possibly legitimate and definitely illegal goods, this task had occupied them at least since Mitch and Bricca had arrived almost two hours before.

In fact they'd been there so long that Mitch was almost looking bored – unless that was just his usual 'worldly New Yorker' expression. It was difficult to tell at this distance, but Adena thought she could see a thread of fear running underneath.

Mitch commented, as if merely making conversation, "I suppose the mothballs throw the dogs in Customs off the scent." Adena could only just hear him, and the acoustics of the space created an odd echo.

"Yes," Bricca replied. "We import espresso coffee this way, too."

"With mothballs?" Mitch looked horrified. Adena had to smile. The man did take his coffee rather seriously.

"With … junk."

Mitch huffed a laugh, and smiled in a pained kind of way. "Coffee with its own sweetener, huh?"

Bricca just cast him a look, and they both fell silent again.

Adena took a moment to consider. She stared at the growing pile of bags of pure white heroin, which glowed eerily under the lights in the otherwise dim warehouse. That decided the matter, as far as she was concerned. She was no clearer about Bricca's intentions for Mitch, but they couldn't just let this play out, not now.

She turned away, crouched further down behind the stack of boxes, and cupped her hand around the radio transmitter before whispering into it. "Nakano. I can see Mitch, Bricca, and five other men towards front of warehouse. They're unpacking what looks like heroin. A whole shitload of it. We need to take them down."

The Man in Black replied over the transmitter, "No."

"You don't understand. There's too much of it. We can't let it reach the streets."

"I told you," he countered, "we're still building a case against Bricca –"

Adena, however, was absolutely determined. "You've got him on bribery and corruption. Probably other stuff you're not telling me. We do this, you've got serious drug-trafficking, too. That's enough."

A long silence stretched. Adena resisted the temptation to argue further. Finally the black-suited man said, "Alright. Give us locations on the targets. You stay on Rebecki. Make sure he doesn't get hurt, but arrest him. Protect his identity."

"Understood." She began, "Bricca's near the west wall, ten meters from the front entrance."

Mitch was waiting for this to be over, though he wasn't quite so desperate as to not be paying attention to detail. Any journalist appreciated learning new things, and often the more unsavory the better.

But then, to his surprise, Mitch glimpsed Adena Nakano creeping along behind the boxes and stuff along one wall, drawing closer to where he and Bricca were standing. The problem was that Mitch was jittery enough to start or maybe flinch a little when he saw her.

And Bricca was too sharp not to pick up on that, of course – so Mitch tried to cover by converting his surprise at Adena to amazement at the growing pile of bags of heroin. He took a couple of steps away from Adena's location and towards the heroin, to distract Bricca visually as well as verbally. "This will be worth tens of thousands, won't it? Hundreds of thousands. What kind of street value are we looking at here?"

"Less than you're thinking," Bricca dryly replied. "The newspapers exaggerate everything."

"It's called sensationalism, it's a job requirement. Anyhow, we just quote the figures that the cops give us."

That amused Bricca. "They have an interest in exaggerating, too."

"Hey, good idea, going to the winery," Mitch commented, wandering towards the pile of unpacked door handles with his hands stuffed in his pockets. "I sure could use a drink after this."

"Patience, Mr. Delmonaco."

There was a faint noise – perhaps Mitch only heard it because he was listening for it, as no one else in his vicinity seemed to. It sounded like a slight scuffle at the front of the building, and then a dead or unconscious guard being lowered to the ground. Trying to cover this, Mitch scuffed a foot across the dusty floor, miming a bored or disconsolate kick, and he retorted, "Patience? I'm a Yank, I don't even know the meaning of the word."

Bricca took a breath as if about to reply – and then he looked about him as if realizing that something was happening – but it was already too late.

The Man in Black, an identically dressed colleague, Jack Wethers, and four uniformed police officers were rushing in, with guns immediately targeting the thugs and Bricca. "Police!" – "Don't move!" – "Don't even think about it!" – "Police! Hands in the air!"

The bad guys froze, took a moment to assess the situation, and then slowly raised their hands.

Mitch just stood there. If his role in this was to act like a dazed and innocent idiot, he felt sure he was doing a fine job.

He was aware that Adena had stood up and shown herself with her gun at the ready as soon as her colleagues appeared. Having approached from a different angle from within the warehouse proper, she was off to one side of the action, close to Mitch and Bricca.

A beat after the others, Adena yelled, "Hands up!"

Mitch didn't realize at first that she was addressing him.

Adena glared, and yelled it again. "Hands up, scumbag!"

Mitch at last did so. He stared hard at her, which he assumed was a fair enough reaction. He was relieved to note that while Adena's gun was ostensibly pointing at him, it was actually aimed safely past him – and in fact seemed quite ready to swing in Bricca's direction.

Speaking of whom … Mitch turned to see that Bricca was thoroughly pissed off by the situation. No doubt he was too used to thinking he was safe from the law. The good guys, with steady efficiency, were fanning out to surround the bad guys. Even so Bricca wasn't standing still, but instead looking restlessly around for ways out. His hands were barely raised and rather than remaining sensibly motionless, his fingers rippled as if desperately wanting to wrap themselves around the butt of a gun.

Taking his cue from Bricca, the dumbest of the thugs belatedly pulled out his own gun.

A shot blasted – louder than Mitch had imagined it could be – and the dumb thug dropped with a damp patch blooming on one shoulder of his dark suit. Jack Wethers seemed to have been the shooter.

But the shot had only pissed off the dumb thug – and the thug's only available target now was Adena – but Adena's attention was on Mitch and

Bricca, and she didn't realize –

Mitch turned, dashed towards her, tackled her to the floor –

The thug's bullet whizzed by just over their heads as they were falling.

But now Mitch and Adena were exposed to Bricca and the rest, and Mitch had made himself a target, too. Adena struggled to disentangle herself, then crouched protectively in front of Mitch. He was chivalrous enough not to like that, but also to appreciate her doing her job. He lay a hand on her waist to guide her as they began edging back towards the nearest pile of boxes while remaining low.

When Mitch glanced up, he saw that Bricca had finally lost his cool, and was glaring furiously at Mitch. Such a betrayal – or outwitting – could not be left unpunished. Bricca reached for his gun –

The other thugs loyally – or stupidly – followed his lead and drew their guns –

Confusion ensued as the bullets flew –

But at last Mitch and Adena made it to cover. Mitch was crouched behind Adena, who stretched back just far enough beyond the boxes to fire two shots, presumably in an effort to dissuade Bricca from following them.

Then, voice strained, she demanded of Mitch, "Are you scared yet?"

"Yes."

"Good. You should be."

Adena fired once more, then settled next to Mitch.

He suddenly saw the blood welling from a wound to her thigh. "Oh God!"

Adena pressed her hand against the wound to try to stanch it, but didn't say anything in response, didn't try to reassure him. Mitch figured that in itself confirmed the thing was serious.

Horrified, Mitch looked around for a moment, trying to think. There was nothing to hand except the two of them and what they had with them. So Mitch pulled off his tie and knotted it around Adena's thigh as a tourniquet. When the blood slowed but kept welling, he shrugged off his jacket – resolutely ignoring the mental reminder that this was one of his best and favorite suits. He bound one of the jacket's arms directly over the wound, and wrapped the rest of the jacket around it as well, then applied pressure with both hands.

Adena winced, but didn't make a sound. She was looking pale, her breath coming hard. She let Mitch take care of her, while occasionally peering around the corner of the box to see what Bricca was doing.

Mitch glanced up as well, to see that Bricca had retreated behind another box that was outside the circle of light, and was returning fire from the other cops. He seemed to be edging towards the better cover where Adena and Mitch were hiding. Adena fired another shot to keep him pinned down. "Mustn't let him past," she said. "There's a back door."

Two of the thugs, and one other cop, were lying dead or injured. Another thug fell even as Mitch watched.

The Man in Black bellowed, "Bricca! Enough! It's over!"

In the sudden quiet, the Man in Black rose from where he'd been sheltering. He had Bricca directly in his sights.

Bricca saw that, and his nerve finally faltered.

The black-suited man took advantage of the moment's grace – he walked towards Bricca, holding his gun steadily on him, taking charge of the situation.

Bricca cried desperately to the thugs, "Shoot him! Shoot him!"

But the remaining bad guys had given up. The cops handcuffed those still standing, and began tending to the wounded. It was over.

Mitch looked down at Adena. She was still pale and grim, but looked no worse than she had. "It's over," he said. "Are you alright?"

"Yes. I'll be fine."

Mitch yelled towards the others, "Hey! We've got an injured cop down here!"

Once he was sure he'd gained Jack's attention, Mitch looked back at Adena. Suddenly he angrily accused, "You took that bullet for me, you idiot."

She replied just as angrily, "Well, you tackled me and blew your cover, moron."

"Yeah, so we're both stupid," he agreed. And then somehow they both let a smile burst through, and they gazed at each other in mutual wonder. "Friends," Mitch said. *Who'd have thought … ?*

"Friends," she agreed.

Mitch could hear a siren in the distance now, which seemed to be drawing closer. "Is that – ?"

"Ambulance."

He nodded. It was going to be O.K.

Mitch stayed with Adena, and even held her hand, until at last she was bandaged, bundled up and strapped onto a gurney, being loaded into an ambulance. Then he had to let her go. Even so, he continued to watch as the ambulance doors were shut, and the vehicle pulled away and smoothly sped down the driveway towards the street. The siren was already blasting.

When he finally turned away, Mitch found that the atmosphere was eerily quiet and subdued as the cops, the black-suited men and the paramedics dealt with the last of the thugs.

A handcuffed Bricca was helped into the back of a police van. He stared coolly at Mitch – the implied threat too obvious and inevitable for Bricca to bother displaying hostility. But Mitch just watched, unconcerned.

In a very real way, it was over. Despite the possibility of retribution, Mitch felt satisfied. He turned and walked away towards where Jack Wethers and the Man in Black were talking things through. There would be witness statements to give, of course, and then Mitch had friends to take care of – and, after that, all would be well.

Twelve

Mitch was at the newspaper offices tapping away at his computer one morning, composing an article for the *Herald* – not about Bricca, not yet. That would have to wait until after the trial. He was, strange to say, smiling.

His smile didn't even falter when the phone rang. He finished a sentence and picked up the handset. "Yeah, Delmonaco here."

"Mitch, it's Tom. From back home in the Big Apple, remember?"

Mitch's smile turned into a grin. "G'day, mate!"

"Oh God, it hasn't been that long, has it?" Tom demanded. "You're talking Strine … You're talking bad Strine with a New York accent. It's pitiful."

"Well, anyway, it's your fault," Mitch argued quite happily. "You sent me here." It occurred to him that he hadn't spoken with Tom for ages. "Hey, have I got a tale for you. We just took down a mobster. Remember that corrupt building company I was telling you about … ?"

"So you've been practicing with the little fish in a little pond, right? I was talking with your guy in the F.B.I., Agent Danes. They're ready to make a move on Cicioni, and Danes actually wants you back here to help out. Not that he exactly put it that way. Bringing Cicioni down was quite the obsession with you, wasn't it … ?"

A silence stretched.

The idea of returning home to New York caught Mitch by surprise. He swung around on his chair to gaze sightlessly out the window. He wasn't unhappy about the prospect, he thought. But there would be things he'd lose by leaving Australia, and the sense of regret was unexpectedly poignant.

"Mitch … ?" Tom eventually asked. "You there?"

"Yeah, I'm here. Uh, so when do you want me?"

"Soon as you can. As soon as Eva can spare you."

"Oh," Mitch said with a laugh, "I don't think *Eva* is going to miss me …"

"Of course not," Tom briskly replied. "Why would she?"

Another silence threatened.

Tom obviously didn't know what to do with that. "Uh, Mitch … ?"

"The timing's good," Mitch said rather slowly. "I annoyed a bad guy not so long ago. I should probably get out of here, change my name, keep my head down."

"How ironic," Tom remarked.

"Look," said Mitch. "I'll call you, O.K.? I'll get some things sorted out, and I'll call you."

"Sure, Mitch. Talk to you soon, mate."

Mitch hung up, but he didn't get back to his story. Instead he stared out the window some more, contemplating.

Mitch told Rory that evening, as they sat on the carpeted steps in the main room of Rory's apartment. Then they both indulged in a bit of 'contemplation while staring out the window'. In the privacy of his own mind, Mitch was very sarcastic about the matter, but that only seemed to provoke further wistfulness. He found himself saying in wretchedly apologetic tones, "We never talked about the long-term, let alone –"

"I know," Rory reassured him with a poignant smile. "But I'll be sad to say goodbye."

Which was apparently the cue for more contemplation.

Perhaps that was the right thing to do, though, because eventually the silence transformed into quietness, and the poignancy became peace.

Mitch said, with simple honesty, "Come to New York sometime. There's a lot of buildings I can show you, incredible buildings."

"I might do that," said Rory, in the same tones. "Some day."

"Yeah, you should. Not because it's better there than here, not because you need it – but because we could do with some of what you've got." Mitch laughed about what an unlikely thing that was for him to say, but God knew how very much he meant it.

The atmosphere lightened. Mitch felt somewhat less stranded, so he shifted closer to Rory, and Rory took one of Mitch's hands in both of his.

"Yeah," Mitch concluded, "you could really shake that place up."

Eva took Mitch to visit Cody's grave, and they quietly paid their respects. Mitch had brought a small but colorful bunch of gerbera daisies, which he felt appropriate for the small but exuberant Cody. He leaned down to place them by her headstone.

Later, when the time was right, Mitch and Eva turned away to contemplate the lovely, dramatic vista of the sea stretching below them and out to the horizon.

Eva remarked, "She has a better view than any of us now."

"I hope so," Mitch replied. Inconsequentially, he added, "She was going to recommend me a novel to read. I guess she never found the right one."

"Perhaps you're better off. Her choice for me hit rather close to home."

After a moment Mitch turned to her. "I have to thank you, Eva. You and Tom have been real friends to me, and I know I never made that easy for anybody."

"*Out of life's school of war*," Eva quoted: "*What does not destroy me, makes me stronger.*"

"Do you really believe that?" Mitch asked.

Eva smiled a little, for maybe the first time since Mitch had met her. "I try to, Mitch. I try to."

Adena was still in hospital, though her main focus now was on rehabilitation. On the day Mitch went to tell her the news, he took her an extravagant bunch of long-stemmed roses in every shade from yellow through orange to pink and red.

The hospital had a half-decent garden, so Mitch went to borrow a wheelchair while Adena shrugged on a robe over her t-shirt and sweat pants, and then they took the elevator down and he wheeled her around as they talked. Inevitably, after discussing Bricca and his fate, and then the current state of play with Rory, Adena asked Mitch how he was feeling about Cody.

"Well, mainly I have regrets," Mitch found himself admitting. He hadn't quite said that before, not even to Eva.

"If Cody thought her life was empty," Adena replied, "she was wrong. But it wasn't your fault, Mitch."

"Oh, there's no need to let me off lightly."

"You've taken it to heart, Mitch. We all know that, and Cody – wherever she is now – knows that, too."

"I could have been a better friend to her. It's not like I didn't empathize."

"When are you going to forgive yourself?" she asked.

"I don't know," he replied with a shrug.

They'd reached a bench. Mitch parked the wheelchair next to it, and then sat down as near to Adena as was reasonable. "Hey, super-cop," he said. "I want to thank you for doing your stuff. I'd be … Well, I wouldn't be going home if it wasn't for you. And we made a great team, didn't we? We got the bad guys! So, thanks."

She was smiling at him. "My pleasure, Mitch."

He glanced down at her bandaged thigh. "Really? Despite ending up in surgery?"

"Yes, really."

Mitch went to take her hand in his, but Adena lifted her arms, and he went with the flow and he *hugged* her.

Mitch sent Rory down to wait with the car so that he could spend his last few minutes in Rory's apartment alone. As a farewell present, Mitch had bought well over twenty picture frames in a range of styles and colors. He arranged them randomly on the floor beneath the wall which currently bore nothing but Rory's wedding photo. Next, Mitch scattered a few photos of Cody's across the frames, including images of Rory and his buildings, and one of Mitch himself. Then he looked around, saw Rory's photo albums in a bookshelf, and brought a random selection of them over. He added coffee-table books featuring the work of Frank Lloyd Wright and Antoni Gaudi.

What Mitch wanted was for Rory to create his own 'wonder wall', adding a bit of context to the lone photo of Rory and Eva. He trusted he'd made that clear. He had his own imaginings of what Rory might do, but of course the best result would be for Rory to create something so very 'him' that Mitch couldn't imagine it at all. Maybe one day Mitch would see the results, but for now all he had was the wish that it might happen.

For a moment Mitch stood back and looked on what he had done with satisfaction. Then he let himself out of the apartment and locked the door behind him.

When Mitch emerged from the apartment building, he found Rory waiting by his MG, with a 'What have you been up to?' expression on his face. Mitch just smiled serenely in reply.

Mitch's two suitcases were already jammed into the boot of the little car. The two men got into the MG, and sped off.

At the airport, Mitch was escorted by Rory as far as he could go, but now they'd reached security, and would finally have to part.

The two men stood there, not knowing quite what to say or do. Mitch felt sad – just as Rory had said he himself would feel sad – though Mitch knew well enough that neither of them was exactly heartbroken. If anything, there was a shared feeling of gladness as well, for what they had managed to be for each other during these past few months. None of which helped Mitch get past this instinctive reluctance to actually walk away.

Announcements and boarding calls were a constant reminder that whatever they wanted to say had better be said soon. People bustled past, a few of them glancing or staring at Rory, recognizing him.

Finally Mitch remarked, "There's one thing I've never had, you know. A big bold passionate farewell at an airport."

Rory regarded him for a moment, and then broke into a mischievous smile. "Is that a dare?"

"Could be."

"Mate, *never* dare an Australian."

And Rory stepped into Mitch's arms, and initiated a wonderfully passionate kiss.

This of course drew some attention, and for a moment or two Mitch wasn't quite so involved that he didn't hear various gasps of disgust or shock, amusement or appreciation. There was even a camera flash, and he wondered if that was an amateur or a professional paparazzo. But then he lost himself in the glorious sensation of being cared for, and long moments passed as the two men reveled in thoroughly farewelling each other.

At last they broke apart. Mitch regretfully pulled away, nodded an acknowledgement, and backed away towards the gates. They didn't say anything more, but they maintained eye contact for as long as possible.

Then Mitch had gone.

Alone again, Rory turned away. But as he walked back through the departure lounge, he found himself beginning to smile. He might have lost Mitch, but Rory figured his life would be quite a bit brighter for having had him for a while.

New York, Spring 2007

Epilogue

Every now and then a perfect spring day dawned. The kitchen in Mitch's Manhattan apartment was still small, but the shafts of gentle sunlight seemed to bring not only light but air and space with them.

Mitch's cork-board was now far more colorful. A few of Cody's photos were tacked up, including one of Rory and one of Adena. There was also one of the selfies that Cody had taken of herself and Mitch during their café crawl. Mixed with these were clippings of Mitch's American and Australian articles, both the newspaper and the glossy supplement stories.

There was one newspaper clipping that wasn't work-related. The photo snapped at the Sydney airport of Mitch and Rory kissing had been sold to a tabloid newspaper, and Mitch had printed it out in all its low-resolution black-and-white glory. It was pinned at the lower right corner of the board with a casualness that even Mitch knew was deceptive.

That day's edition of the *New York Times* was lying on the table where Mitch had left it. The front page featured an article with the Mitch Rebecki byline and a headline triumphantly announcing *CICIONI INDICTED*.

Mitch eventually walked in, having returned from collecting his very own stray black cat. He placed the cat's traveling cage on the table, talking with her all the while, as if answering her complaints. "I don't know why they didn't quarantine me, too." He indicated his high forehead. "Maybe it's because I don't have as much fur as you."

He fetched out the new pet food dishes, poured water into one and set it in the old familiar place. "Cheer up," he said to the cat, "it wasn't for *that* long."

He served some food into the other dish – food that was as close as he could find to what the cat had liked in Sydney. And then finally he undid the cage, and lifted out the cat. He held her in his arms and stroked her for a few moments, and then set her down on the bench by the window.

The cat looked around suspiciously, crouched as if ready to spring away. Mitch hoped she wouldn't try to dash out the cat-flap, but figured drawing her attention to it by blocking it would do more harm than good.

She cast a doubting glance at Mitch, then looked around again in disgruntlement.

"No, it's just me here, I'm afraid."

But finally the cat settled down and tucked into the food, apparently content enough.

Mitch smiled. "Welcome home, Pulitzer Too."

He stood there propped against the bench, keeping the cat company. He had to admit he was feeling pretty damned content himself, though there was as always much to wish for. What would life be, however, without something to strive for?

His smile dimmed a little as Mitch said to the cat, "You know that Cicioni's new lieutenant managed to escape the net, right? He's who we'll focus on next, I think. Nothing's ever quite perfectly finished, is it?"

And then Mitch started as the phone rang – his land-line, which no one ever called. He actually looked around, having to remember where it was. The ring tone continued, patiently or maybe determinedly waiting for him to answer.

After a moment, Mitch went over and picked up the handset. "Hello?"

"Mitch? Mitch, it's Rory. Rory Pierce," he added, as if Mitch might have forgotten him.

Mitch was grinning happily. He hadn't forgotten anything at all.

"Are you there … ? Hello?"

And Mitch finally replied, "Oh, Rory …" It was *so* good to hear the man. "G'day, mate!"

Content Warning

This story includes the on-page death by **suicide** of a significant secondary character, and the grief and confusion experienced by the character's friends. *Please do not read this if you feel it may do you harm.*

In thinking about why I felt compelled to include this storyline, I haven't come up with anything more succinct than the following quote from the film *The Hours* (Stephen Daldry, 2002).

In the relevant scene, Virginia Woolf is writing her novel *Mrs. Dalloway*, which includes the suicide of the character Septimus Warren Smith, a traumatized veteran of the First World War. Leonard Woolf queries this, asking why someone in the novel must die.

Virginia replies, "Someone has to die in order that the rest of us should value life more. It's contrast."

The lesson is not lost on her Mrs. Dalloway – nor on my Mitch Rebecki. I trust that a character's death in a fictional story is enough of a lesson for the rest of us.

If you or someone you know is feeling suicidal, *please seek help*.
>   In **Australia**:
>   Suicide Call Back Service 1300 659 467
>   Lifeline 13 11 14
>   Kids Helpline 1800 55 1800
>   In the **United Kingdom**:
>   Samaritans 116 123
>   Childline 0800 1111
>   Silver Line (for older people) 0800 4 70 80 90
>   In the **United States**:
>   National Suicide Prevention Lifeline 1-800-273-TALK (8255)
>   Veterans / Military Crisis Line 1-800-273-8255 Press 1
>   Crisis Text Line 741-741

About Julie Bozza

Ordinary people are extraordinary. We can all aspire to decency, generosity, respect, honesty – and the power of love (all kinds of love!) can help us grow into our best selves.

I write stories about 'ordinary' people finding their answers in themselves and each other. I write about friends and lovers, and the families we create for ourselves. I explore the depth and the meaning, the fun and the possibilities, in 'everyday' experiences and relationships. I believe that embodying these things is how we can live our lives more fully.

Creative works help us each find our own clarity and our own joy. Readers bring their hearts and souls to reading, just as authors bring their hearts and souls to writing – and together we make a whole.

I read books, lots of books, and watch films. I admire art, and love theatre and music. I try to be an awesome partner, sister, daughter, friend. I live an engaged and examined life. And I strive to write as honestly as I can.

I have lived in two countries – England and Australia – which has helped widen my perspective, and I have travelled as well. I love learning, and have completed courses in all kinds of things. My careers have been in Human Resources, and in eLearning and training, so there has always been a focus on my fellow human beings and on understanding, conveying, sharing information.

Knitting gives me some down time and the chance to craft something with my hands. Coffee gives me stimulation and a certain street cred. My favourite colour has segued from pure blue to dark purple, and seems to be segueing again to marine blues.

I think John Keats is the best person who has ever lived.

And that's me! Julie Bozza. Quirky. Queer. Sincere.

If you want to know more, please do come find me at **juliebozza.com** and **libra-tiger.com**.

Titles by Julie Bozza

The Butterfly Hunter Trilogy:
     Butterfly Hunter
     Of Dreams and Ceremonies
     Like Leaves to a Tree
     The Thousand Smiles of Nicholas Goring

Albert J. Sterne:
     The Definitive Albert J. Sterne
     Albert J. Sterne: Future Bright, Past Imperfect

Novels and Novellas:
     The Apothecary's Garden
     The Fine Point of His Soul
     Homosapien … a fantasy about pro wrestling
     Mitch Rebecki Gets a Life
     A Night with the Knight of the Burning Pestle
     A Threefold Cord
     The 'True Love' Solution
     The Valley of the Shadow of Death

Stories and Anthologies:
     Call to Arms
     A Certain Persuasion
     Crisis at Christmas
     An English Heaven
     No Holds Bard
     A Pride of Poppies